RATHCROG

A Horror Novel

By Neil T. Jacobs

Acknowledgments

My thanks to Denis Hamel for his willingness to share his knowledge and experience as a police officer, and to former Groton, MA Deputy Chief of Police, James Cullen for his time and information. Any liberties I have taken or errors that exist in this book related to police procedures are entirely my responsibility.

A special thanks to Wendy Lady for your feedback, advice, and editing prowess - sorry about the nightmares.

To my beloved wife and patient partner, Amie – thanks for putting up with me.

and

To my three amazing children, Elizabeth, Samantha, and Michael – you have kept me young.

At this point, I'm only missing an accordion.

Chapter 1

God damn bugs.

Dennis Tierney was not fond of insects. Or sweating. Or, at the moment, West Virginia. But here he was, starting over, following the humiliating end to his marriage.

Fucking bitch.

Finding his wife in bed with someone else was bad enough. Worse was finding her in a tangled heap with his dental assistant, with whom he had been having an affair for the previous six months.

He pushed the image out of his mind, but not before sending a *fucking dykes* thought north to Bridgett, his former New Hampshire residence.

He spotted a large rock jutting up from the ground and perched on it as he pulled out the handwritten map and traced the path he had already made from the old logging road a few miles back. The best he could tell, the town shouldn't be more than another quarter mile.

He got up and continued his walk, giving his forehead another swipe with his sweaty bandana as he kicked through vines that crossed what had probably been an unpaved truck route or possibly a wagon trail at some point in the past.

Better be worth it.

He had learned of the old mining town earlier in the week at the after-hours Chamber of Commerce mixer as he chatted with Carl Miller, long-retired owner of the biggest, and only, insurance firm in town. After mentioning his plan to visit the Prescott Town Museum, out of boredom more than any interest in piss-ant local history, Carl had snorted.

"Don't bother. It's crap. Aside from a few Indian arrowheads and a plaque with an extremely suspect claim that Davy Crockett stayed a night in town once, there isn't anything worthwhile seeing. Hell, there isn't anything worth seeing in Prescott now."

"What about during the time of King Coal? I know that's long gone now, but I would have thought—"

Carl interrupted, "More hogwash from our illustrious Chamber President." He gestured across the room where Pamela Hotchkins was scanning name badges at the welcome table. Along with running the local chamber, she was also the proprietor of the Prescott Inn and town mayor. Like most small towns, including the one Dennis escaped from, you had to make your own opportunities if you wanted to get by.

She seemed to sense their looks and glanced at them. She gave a brief smile and ducked her head again, a faint blush on her cheeks.

Dennis had been playing verbal footsie with her for weeks. While his ex-wife might have considered his dental skills mediocre, his salesmanship was generally quite effective, particularly as it related to getting invited into women's beds. But while he had made progress with the chamber-inn-town-running Ms. Hotchkins, she had yet to invite him. He could ask her back to his place, but he had a rule. *They* had to ask *him*. It was a clear sign they were at a sufficiently malleable emotional point. Besides, he enjoyed the hunt. Once he had a target in sight, it usually didn't take more than a couple of get-togethers - a few drinks here, a quiet dinner there - before there would be a shy request asking him to join her. He had stopped being surprised that most had bedrooms decorated in a combination pseudo-Victorian combined with emotionally stunted teenage motif–stuffed animals, pastel curtains and sheets, heavy on flowers and pink, four-poster beds shrouded with scarves.

Damaged goods - he could smell them from twenty paces.

He was sure Hotchkins was of the same ilk, but he was into personal overtime at this point and wondered if he was losing his touch. Which reminded him of his cunt of an ex-wife, Amanda, and her lover, his traitorous former assistant, Carol.

Fucking dykes.

It was practically a mantra now.

He pushed the thought away and focused on Pamela Hotchkins' ass. Not the best, but it would do. Help get him out of his slump, at least. She was in her late thirties, a few years older than him, but still acceptable. The pickings were rather slim in Prescott.

He was sure she wanted him. He couldn't be that far off his game. From their first conversation, when he had called the Chamber responding to a Dental Association email ad with the headline, 'Subsidies Available for Select Professionals Interested in Relocating to Beautiful West Virginia - See What We Have to Offer!' she had been flirtatious in a demure, country-girl sort of way. By the end of the conversation, he had decided two things. That Prescott was at least better than staying in Bridgett where within hours everyone knew about his humiliation, and that he would be letting the chamber president take him home, assuming she wasn't a two-bagger, or worse.

But so far, she hadn't invited him in. After their last date, with his charm turned to eleven, they had ended up on her front steps for an extended face sucking and a bit of titty play. Based on experience and the little sounds she made, he was sure she would finally cave.

But she had finally pulled away and, once again, he found himself unable to break the threshold of her small Cape Cod, or her. Something was holding her back. Maybe—His reverie was interrupted as Carl continued, not noticing the woman's blush. "Ever since she became mayor, Pamela's been on a quest to rebuild Prescott to what she calls its *former glory*." The old man took a sip from his whiskey and soda. "Only problem is, it never had a glory. We were a spin-off from Warner."

"Warner?" The name didn't ring a bell. "I don't remember any Warner around the area. Am I misremembering?"Another snort. "No, you're not. I would be surprised if you had heard of it. There hasn't been a Warner since the nineteen twenties."

"It was a mining town?"

"Oh yes," Carl nodded, clinking his ice with the swizzle stick. "The first shaft was dug in the eighteen eighties and by the time the town was abandoned, there were three. Forrester Mining built the town for workers and owned it: lock, stock, and barrel. Prescott was a come-behind. Mostly hangers-on. Brothels, bars, not that there was any difference back then, grocers, and the like."

"What happened?"

The old man shrugged.

"The first two mines were just about tapped out but still in operation, from what the stories say, and number three hit a wall of water shortly after opening, something initial surveys apparently didn't show. Not long after, Forrester picked up its balls and moved out of state."

"So, Warner is still there. Just sitting empty?"

He wasn't particularly interested in history. His planned museum trip was more to take a break from spending yet another day off sitting at the local watering hole rather than any deep curiosity about Prescott. One shithole town was the same as any other, as he could attest from lifelong experience.

But the idea of a ghost-town nearby, and one that wasn't even mentioned in the Chamber flyers that touted anything that might even potentially give someone a reason to visit the area, sounded at least moderately distracting. Tully's Tavern, and the divorcées that spent their own off-time sipping margaritas waiting for Mr. At-Least-Not-A-Total-Loser to buy them another round could wait. Neither was going anywhere.

Carl nodded somewhat distractedly, eyes on the far wall of the Chamber conference room. He was either lost in thought or, more likely in Dennis's opinion, half-crocked.

He prompted the retiree again. "Carl?"

The older man pulled his eyes back to the dentist, returning to the conversation from wherever he had been.

"Last I knew, anyway. Kids have been going out there for years. Me included back in the day."

"The buildings, or what's left of them, are still there, mostly taken over by kudzu and knotweed at this point." He paused to take a sip of his drink. "I went out once, homecoming weekend with a few friends and a case of beer. That was enough..." He trailed off.

"What?" Dennis asked. "See a ghost?" He chuckled at his own joke.

Carl gave a nervous laugh in return and finished his whiskey in one large gulp.

"Oh, nothing. Drunk teenager memories. There have been a lot of stories cooked up over the years." He peered at Dennis and turned serious. "I can see you're thinking about making a trip out there. I won't tell you not to. Enough people have. But I will strongly recommend you get back to the county road before it gets dark. The buildings themselves aren't in good shape, whatever is left of them. The shafts, at least, are blocked off. Also, it's easy to get lost in those woods, even for someone who grew up around here."

He nodded in agreement at the suggestion and asked if Carl could give him directions.

"I can give you basic directions. But first," he held up his glass, a few lonely ice cubes shaking emptily in it, "you can buy me another of these." He grinned. "When you get to my age, you need all the help you can get remembering things."

<hr>

To his left, he saw jumbled stones showing the rough outline of a foundation. The trees were thinning as well. And was that a chimney further up ahead? Yes, it definitely was.

He kept moving. A lack of appointments allowed him to close his office at noon, and although he had started his trip just after one, it was well past four now. Although the retiree's map was generally accurate, he had either played fast and loose with distances or that last drink had fogged his memory more than Dennis had thought it had.

He stepped out from the trees onto gravel.

Finally.

Spread across his field of view were low-lying buildings in various states of decay, most partially obscured by vines. Some had trees growing up through where roofs had once kept the elements out. Even after almost a hundred years, though, he could tell it had been a busy, if condensed, town. As he carefully made his way into what he assumed was the start of the downtown, signs advertising rooms, groceries, supplies, and drink (these outnumbered all others by a factor of four) dotted the landscape on both sides. He paused in front of a storefront with a half-fallen sign proclaiming *Long's Laundry - Fast Service!* He smoothed the napkin with Carl's wavery scrawl across it as best he could against his leg and traced the spidery ink through the town. Down to the end of what was Main Street and then west an unknown bit should be the run-up to shaft number three, if Carl hadn't been too buzzed by the time he scrawled the note. Number three had been the final one, opened not long before Warner had imploded.

He didn't know why he had badgered the man to tell him where it was. He supposed it was just the slight pique of interest in Warner that he felt. Aside from pussy, which was a given, he hadn't been particularly interested in anything since arriving in Prescott.

His plan was to find a couple of souvenirs during his outing, maybe a pickaxe or miner's helmet. He assumed Pamela was familiar with Warner at least peripherally, since she had grown up in the area. Presenting her with a tidbit of local history, maybe something she could incorporate into a chamber flyer, might be the final piece in piercing...well, her.

He turned left onto West Street, so identified by the askew sign hanging from the corner building. The buildings tapered off then just stopped, a couple of wagons and the skeletons of a few trucks just past them and...was that it? It was, indeed. Metal tracks, narrower than what could support a train, ran between the husks, up to a large metal gate.

Good for you, Carl. Not too fucking drunk to scribble a map.

The trucks appeared to be held together by rust; the wagons were miniature gardens of tall yellow and black flowers, more blooms cascading over their sides.

He was surprised that he hadn't seen a similar arrangement in anyone's front yard around town.

Scanning the truck beds for a souvenir-cum-bribe, he saw only scattered leaves, dirt, and more rust. He picked up a stick and was poking at the detritus, thinking that maybe something worth hauling back was buried underneath, when he heard it.

He turned his head from one side to the other as he dug his finger into his ear. It was more a vibration, almost but not quite a buzzing. A *thrumming*. He felt it in his tailbone, then in his balls.

It was almost comforting.

He turned from the truck, head still tilted, when faint bells overlaid the buzzing.

The sky had dulled with the approaching sunset, and something nudged a corner in his mind. Something about sunset. But the thrumming grew, and the nudging dissipated. He walked a circle around the trucks and wagons, trying to find where exactly it was coming from.

The shaft.

He studied the gate. Flaking metal on the bars that extended across the blocked-up opening, thick wooden pillars framing the gates. He dropped the stick and approached.

As he did, he shook his head again. The thrumming was tickling through his ears down to his throat.

There was a padlock on the gate, rusty but intact.

Bzzzz

He yanked on it, but the heavy metal didn't budge.

The thrumming in his head increased.

Shzzzz

He kicked at the lock.

Nothing.

He turned to the trucks and picked up the stick again.

Snap

The old wood broke as soon as he applied pressure to it.

A current traveled up one side of his jawline.

His head snapped to the left of the gate. Scrub brush grew up the side of the hill. Bending over, he started pulling it up, not noticing or feeling the narrow slices and holes the prickers left behind; small dots of blood formed on his hands and lower arms. With the plants cleared, he clawed into the mounded rocks, dirt, and sand. Another slice, this one deeper, as his right hand ran up against metal. He dug more and was able to pull the buried pickax free by its dirt-crusted wooden handle. The head was covered in rust but seemed solid.

Panting now, he stood again in front of the gate and wedged the curved metal through the center of the lock. His breath puffed as he leaned into it, but the lock still didn't give. Again and again, arms straining, he tried to pry the lock open, but it held fast.

He slapped his head as the buzzing intensified and walked back to one of the wagons, which listed to its side where a wooden axle dug into the ground. Crouching, he crawled halfway under the bed and used both hands to pull the stone out, then wiggled backwards; one pants leg tore on a small, jagged stone, leaving a quarter-sized hole gouged into his skin.

He lugged the rock and set it down for a moment at the gate, his sweat flowing heavily. The pick still hung, wedged through the U of the lock clasp. Grunting with the effort, he lifted the stone over his head and brought it down on the handle of the axe.

With a *chunk,* the lock dropped to the ground.

The gate, a century's worth of build-up gumming its hinges, remained closed. He stood for a moment, then reached out and pulled on it.

It opened in groaning spurts as he jerked on it, and when he finally had it pulled all the way back, he stared at the piles of rock and dirt behind it, blocking what once had been the entrance.

He grabbed the pickaxe and began digging.

Chapter 2

Carl regretted telling Dennis about Warner the other night.
But then, he regretted a lot of things. Not having been a
good enough husband to notice the lump on his wife's breast.
Not having taken his brother-in-law's recommendation in '98
to buy stock in an upstart internet shopping company (he
remembered arguing with Fred that people would never want
to buy much of anything through the computer; much easier
to just pop down to a local store). And, right now, especially,
that fourth whiskey he cajoled Dennis into buying him before
he scribbled out his best, inebriated remembrance of how to
get to Warner.

*What harm? We all went out there, once upon a time. It was
a rite of passage. Something to impress the girls. I spent the night
in Warner!*

But he hadn't, really. And to his knowledge, no one else ever
had either. In the woods, at a safe distance, yes. A quarter mile,
half mile. It depended on how much liquid courage one had.
He couldn't remember how much he had drunk that night,

but between him, Corey, and Tusker, they had polished a case of Jax off before passing out in the back of Corey's father's Chevy C20, parked way back down the old road that had connected Warner to the rest of the world.

He dropped his clothes onto the straight-back chair in a corner of the room, scratched his ass, and climbed into bed, thinking back to that night so many years ago, as he had been doing regularly since the chamber mixer. The memory was something he had shied away from over the years, both subconsciously and, at times, consciously. Regina, his wife, had grown up in Morgantown so had considered the occasional mention of the mining town by Prescott old-timers so many will-o'-the-wisps. But he had never spoken to her about that night, although she knew he had gone through the standard Prescott coming of age Warner-night.

He settled under the quilt given them by an aunt on their wedding day, reached a hand over to pat Regina's pillow as he did every night, and guided his mind back to 1946.

His father had been back from Korea only a few weeks. The man who arrived at the two-bedroom cabin, though, was not the same smiling father Carl remembered from a few years prior. A quiet stranger with a slight twitch in one eye and a tendency to jump if his mother set down the supper dishes too hard had taken his place. Carl was graduating in another week and, although he would continue to live at home while he attended the state college in Morgantown, driving two hours each way, he would be free to come and go, mostly go, his own way.

He, Corey Edwards, and Lou 'Tusker' Hammond, friends since grade school, headed out in Ed Edwards' flatbed. Buying the beer hadn't been a problem. It was a long-established tradition that any of the usual questions that might arise from teenage boys purchasing alcohol were put aside in the week leading up to graduation. By eight o'clock that night, the three had been quite drunk, slap-wrestling, telling dirty-jokes and ghost stories, filling the time between chugs from the slowly warming cans.

And as the beer disappeared, each took their turn, pushing the others to move the truck closer and closer to the town. By the time the last of the beer had been drunk and Tusker and Corey had settled into respective corners of the truck bed, blankets pulled up around them, they were at the end of the old entrance road, the Chevy's nose a few feet from the cracked pavement that signified arrival in Warner.

He hadn't been able to sleep. He was bleary-eyed from the evening's festivities, but his mind seemed to be a jumble of thoughts that wouldn't settle down. The changes in his father. Stories about Warner. Going off to college.

He climbed over the tailgate and dropped lithely to the ground, his bladder ready to burst. As he relieved himself under a white pine, he felt something brush by his ear. He reached up and swiped at it with his free hand, but felt nothing. Business finished, he executed the standard three shakes, which common wisdom mandated was the maximum number else you were diddling yourself.

A tingle ran up his legs.

He jumped, thinking a weevil was out past its bedtime, but when he reached down and shook his pants, there was nothing.

He buttoned the trousers and cursed himself for his jumpiness.

Too many ghost stories.

The woods were quiet. No owl calls, no skittering across fallen branches. Not even cicadas, which were back in this part of the state as part of their seventeen-year cycle. That, more than the quick dance across his skin, unnerved him more than anything else.

Tusker and Corey were both snoring softly when he returned to the truck. Tusker's fist was up against his buck-toothed mouth, and he was making a sucking sound, something that Carl would rib him about the next morning. As he climbed back into the bed, the tingling returned, this time running through his legs, then throughout his entire body. He felt like he was covered in exposed wires. But it wasn't just the tingling. There was a *push* inside his head.

A demanding.

What?

He had jumped back out of the truck and now turned in a slow circle, stopping when he faced toward the town.

His hips pulled forward, almost causing him to fall, his feet trying to keep up.

Zhmmm

The tingling was gone, replaced by a humming in his head. He shook it, feeling like a bee's nest had been let loose inside his skull. He tried to think through it, but the harder he tried, the louder the humming got.

Of their own volition, his legs started a slow, awkward lumber down the length of the truck. He made a single attempt to halt his steps, but the buzzing turned into a buzz saw and he was blinded by bright white flashes. His legs, though, needed no guidance, and continued forward. As soon as he gave up arguing with his body, the buzzing dropped to a tolerable volume and the light faded. A voice came through the noise as he passed the front bumper.

"Carl? Hey, Carl, where you goin'?"

The noise cut off completely. It took a moment to realize he could think, and Carl stopped walking and turned back toward the truck.

"Tusker?"

"Yeah." The freckled eighteen-year-old leaned unsteadily against the back of the truck cab.

Carl lifted a leg experimentally and felt no resistance. He walked the few feet back to stand, looking up at Tusker.

"Did you hear something?"

"No," came the reply. "Jus' 'bout pissed me...myself. Thas' what woke me up." He climbed down, took a few steps to the rear of the vehicle, and let loose a stream that would have done Seabiscuit proud. Buttoning his pants, he peered up through the branch canopy over the rutted path. "What time s'it?"

"Uh...probably one o'clock or so." Carl tried looking at his watch but couldn't read the dial in the forest darkness.

"Don' know I've ev...ever been up this late b'fore,' Tusker replied, trying to pull himself back into the truck. "Where were you goin', anyway?"

"Nowhere," he said and shoved his friend up and over the wooden rails running around the bed. "Couldn't sleep so I was just pacing a bit." Apparently, Tusker hadn't heard, or felt, anything, and now that he was past it, Carl told himself he had either been having a waking dream or had been sleepwalking.

He pulled himself up and settled into another corner, noticing that Tusker had collapsed back into his own nest, out already. He took his jacket off and bundled it into a rough pillow-shape. Head propped on it, he made himself think about graduation and Kelly Armitrage's legs in her cheerleading outfit.

But it was a long time before he fell asleep. And the dreams that followed were not happy ones.

<hr>

As Carl's mind traveled back to that long ago night, his hands gripped the quilt unconsciously, mimicking his younger self pulling his jacket tight. Not for the first time, he wondered if he really had imagined the experience.

Of course I did. Ghost stories and beer. That's all it was.

But still.

All the stories said that the first two shafts had about been tapped out and when the mine company unexpectedly hit water in the third, Forrester packed it in and moved on to greener, or blacker, pastures. Some place they had just started pulling from up in Ohio. Or was it Illinois? Either way, they had offered to relocate any worker that wanted to follow them, guaranteeing them a job on the other end.

He had never questioned the story. Being honest with himself, something he generally avoided, self-examination not being conducive to growing an insurance business, he had studiously tried to not think about Warner, or that night, except when the shroud of a dream took a few moments to dissolve in early morning light. But as worry about Dennis nibbled at him, he made himself consider.

Assuming the story about the relocation offer was true (which in itself stretched credibility; more likely it was something circulated by Warner PR people), had he ever known anyone around Prescott that claimed to have family that worked at the mines? Had he even *heard* of anyone that had a father, grandfather, any relative that had?

He searched his memory. Like most small towns, Prescott was big on multi-generational families, newcomers making up a very small percentage of its population at any given time. Surely, at least growing up, he must have known someone.

A dozen old-time family names ran through his head, including Tusker's and Corey's, both of which were farm families. He discarded each as he mentally identified occupations.

Old Willie Frasier? No, he worked on Warner trucks before he switched to the County, but they brought the trucks to him, out at his place on Pheasant. Pat Larkins' father? Maybe, but both Sr. and Jr. are dead. He remembered attending Pat Jr.'s wake.

Didn't he have a daughter, though? Meredith Larkin? Wait, she got married, widowed now. Tom Baxter, so Meredith Baxter.

She had moved, he remembered, but just out to Banyon Lake, a few miles from Prescott and abutting the old border of Warner. Maybe he could...

A frisson ran up his body and he jumped in bed. A faint humming wafted through the room.

His first impulse was to pull the blanket up over his head, like a child trying to hide, but cursed himself for his foolishness.

You're old and jumping at shadows.

Yes, but this shadow he had felt, or heard, before. He pulled the faded covering off and sat up stiffly. He waited a moment before standing and wished he had taken a couple of Motrin before turning in.

The room, house, and street were quiet. He would have written off the experience to alcohol and memory-induced overly stimulated emotions but for the familiarity.

He pulled back the curtains and looked out at the small, fenced backyard. There was nothing moving.

What the hell have I done?

If he had thought about it, Dennis would have been surprised at the good shape the tunnel was in, thick wooden support beams not showing any damage or wear, and at the scattered equipment. Digging tools, helmets, and even a pair of thick-soled boots littered his path downward. But his buzzing mind had room for only one semi-coherent thought - to find the source. Or rather, SOURCE, so important was the goal. Upon entering the tunnel, a tingling wave had run across his skin, leaving behind dime-sized goosebumps.

He also had a raging erection.

His eyes had just grown accustomed to the dusty haze-light filtering from the tunnel opening when the path jogged right, and he found himself in total blackness. It didn't matter. Eyes weren't needed here. Independent of sight, his brain and his body played a game of hot-cold, walking by side-passages he knew to be dead-ends or not along the path to his ultimate destination. He came upon a three-tined fork and waited a moment until the bones in his left arm vibrated, then turned down the left-most passage. He stepped neatly around more mining tools, which had partially decomposed and desiccated bodies scattered amongst them. The corpses varied in size and dress and if he had had an eye for anything except the path ahead, he would have noticed there appeared to be children and women along with miners.

It was well past nine now, and the air was colder and damper, but he had no concept of time or place. What he did know, or sense, was that he was close. Wiry hairs on his scrotum were trying to stand up and his sack was as tight as when he mounted a new conquest.

There.

The tunnel ran up a ramp of loose stones which ended in a former opening, blocked by soil and rocks. He still had the pickaxe with him and went to work. Shortly, a faint glow came through the opening he had made, and he looked upon a large, open cavern. His already blistered hands had large flaps of skin hanging and blood seeped from the open wounds. Ignoring them, he continued clearing until the opening was large enough to stoop through.

Walls extended thirty or more feet above the cavern, forming a dome overhead. The wall opposite him was at least a football field distant. In the center of the cave he saw it.

The SOURCE.

He shuffled to the water and dropped to his knees, hands dipping into its stillness. He ignored three bodies, these worn to skeletons by the damp air, lying nearby.

The disturbance his bloody hands made on the water's surface sent an ever-widening ripple outward as he brought a double handful toward his mouth.

The first swallow was like a flash flood rushing down a steep hardpan gulley, leaving no trace, and his thirst grew as though alive within him. As he leaned forward, the water seemed to take on a glow. Sticking his head under the warm water, he gulped as quickly as he could, staying under until his body could no longer fight his lungs' craving for oxygen. His head had not quite cleared the surface when he inhaled, and he rolled to his side, coughing and spewing liquid.

He lay on his back in the quiet, staring at the water-lit stone ceiling, breath slowing from a pant. His heart took on a steady *thud- thud* as the thrumming traveled over, through, and under his flesh from his feet to his scalp. A quick tug and his belt came loose. He shimmied his pants down his waist, struggling to free his hardness and, with a roughness he had never allowed a woman, he began masturbating. After a few seconds, hand still sliding up and down, he used his feet and ass to pull himself closer to the edge. Feet hanging down into the water, his hiking boots filled quickly.

Yes, Oh Yes!

By the time he had cum, there was blood trickling out from between his fingers.

As the sun broke the horizon, he was tired, but it was a good kind of tired.

Good night's work, he thought, loading two jugs into the back of his SUV before getting in. He would have to come back later in the day, but had at least made a start. He couldn't remember when the local hardware store opened on Saturdays but wasn't concerned since he had a stop to make first.

His crusted reddish-brown hands stuck to the wheel as he drove toward Prescott. While he generally liked to crank the radio while he drove, the buzzing in his head was more than enough accompaniment for the trip back into town.

Chapter 3

Pamela Hotchkins was just finishing her blueberry muffin and tea in the Inn kitchen when the front desk bell rang three times in quick succession. She wasn't expecting a check-in today. There were no guests at the moment, which was often the case and one reason she had taken on the Chamber presidency. Not that anyone else had shown an interest upon the death of her predecessor. Her petite form moved hurriedly through the swinging doors from the kitchen into the dining room, then through the front parlor to the counter.

"Dennis?"

It wasn't a question of identity. Rather, she was taken aback by his appearance. She had never seen him dressed in anything her grandmother wouldn't have classified as 'natty' when she was a young girl. Not in a suit, necessarily, but always at least casually professional. And clean.

The man standing at the counter was neither. His button-down shirt was untucked and had large dirt spots on it. His jeans had tears in them, surrounded by dark stains. The boots he wore were filthy and had spots the same color as the ones on his pants. A large plastic jug dangled from a grimy hand.

The smell of sweat permeated the air around him.

He smiled at her.

"Hi Pamela. Wanted to show you something."

"Are you all right?"

She had enjoyed their dates and had been tempted more than once to ask him to accompany her back to one of the empty guest rooms, perhaps even her own room. Their last outing, a romantic dinner at Sargasson's Italian Bistro, had almost pushed her over the edge. The half bottle of wine she had drunk kept murmuring "do it" but as much as she was attracted to him, her grandmother's admonitions kept rolling through her head. By old-fashioned standards, she was well into permanent spinsterhood at thirty-six. By current standards, her virginity was something she would not have mentioned even to close friends, if she had had any.

So, when he drove her home, and after a few minutes on the front porch acting like teenagers at the drive-in, she had disengaged, thanked him for the evening, and went in alone. She had drawn a warm bath and slid her fingers beneath the sudsy water. Even then, she could hear Nana's voice from the one time her grandmother had caught her touching herself, screaming how she was going to Hell.

But it didn't stop her and when she was done, she thought back over the evening.

He had been respectful, as always, which endeared him to her even more.

Such a gentleman. Next time.

She knew how foolish it was, saving herself for something that might never come. But early lessons weren't easy to shrug off, especially when those lessons were emphasized with a length of hickory as thick as a man's thumb.

She had occasional dreams of herself in white, walking down the aisle, Dennis waiting, that lovely smile of his and she would awaken, thinking *Maybe it will come....*

But now, he looked more like a dockworker, or miner, than a gentleman. He stood, a different sort of smile on his face, close-lipped, rocking side to side as though enjoying a song only he could hear.

"Dennis, I asked if you were ok?"

"Right as rain," he finally replied. "Do you have a couple of glasses?"

"Um...glasses?"

He held up the jug.

"Sure. We could drink straight from the bottle, but that's a bit low-class, don't you think?"

"Is it moonshine?"

His laugh was so pure she found herself smiling back, regardless of the strangeness of the situation.

"Of course not. You know me. A glass or two of wine with a beautiful woman over dinner, but that's it."

She laughed. With a shake of her head, she motioned for him to follow her back toward the kitchen.

"What have you been getting into, you crazy man?" It occurred to her that this was the perfect time to talk to him, explain things. No guests, nowhere to be. Maybe today was the day…

A hand on her arm twirled her around and she found herself pushed against the dining room wall.

"Wha—?"

His lips were against hers, his body tight up against her robe. The stink of his sweat was almost overpowering.

"Hmmph," she mumbled, pushing back against his chest, but not before meeting his tongue briefly, indicating she wasn't against the kiss, simply the timing.

As she broke away, regretfully as warmth spread through her body, she said, "Whew. Mr. Tierney, you are quite the handful this morning." He started to reply, but she put her finger up to his lips. "But I need to talk to you first. And perhaps you could use my shower to clean up. Whatever you've been up to—"

He pushed his face back into hers and she shoved harder. The warmth spread, but Nana's voice was in her head again and she turned her head.

Mumbling into his cheek, she said, "Dennis, darling, please! I…I want you, too. I think you know that. But we really should talk first. There are things I need to tell you."

For a moment she felt tenseness in his body and wasn't sure he would listen, but then he eased back slightly with a look that sent a shiver up her back.

Another tight-lipped smile. "Sure thing, Pamela. Of course." He stepped back further, gave an exaggerated bow, and motioned toward the swinging doors.

She smiled back, thankful he understood.

He is a sensitive man, she thought as she made her way back into the kitchen. *We will do his toast and he will tell me what he has going on. Maybe he's expanding his business? Then, we'll talk and after…*

She took down two water glasses from the cupboard, but he said, "No, wine glasses. It's a celebration."

She gave him a bemused look but nodded and swapped them for long-stem crystal, left to her by Nana.

He took the cap off the jug and took them one at a time from her, pouring a few inches into each.

He raised his to her as she asked, "What are we toasting? New business venture?" She swirled the contents of her glass as she looked into his gray-blue eyes.

His fine, white teeth showed this time when he smiled, and she had the oddest thought.

Shark.

"To new beginnings," he said, answering her first question, and downed the liquid.

She hesitated a moment, smiled back and held her glass aloft before drinking its contents.

Carl fidgeted, feeling foolish. He looked out his windshield at the trailer. A tilted burned-out wooden frame over by the woods to one side of the trailer spoke to a previous conflagration; the weeds growing up and through it a sign the blaze had occurred some time ago.

When he had pulled into the driveway, guarded by a rooster-shaped mailbox with 'Larkins' handwritten on its side, he had stopped for a moment and considered going back home and having a drink. That would be a much better way to spend a Saturday afternoon than this foolish trip. The early hour wouldn't bother him in the least if he began imbibing. His definition of appropriate times for a cocktail had gotten progressively more flexible since Regina's death. Some days, he worked on what he called 'China Time', as they were a good twelve hours ahead of West Virginia.

Instead, he had promised himself a double later and put the car back into drive, making his way down the quarter mile of gravel road. He pulled up next to an older sedan with a garbage bag taped in place of one of the back windows.

What are you doing?

Damned if he knew.

Pat Larkins Jr. had been dead a good eight years. He had met his daughter, Meredith, in the receiving line at the wake, but that was the extent of his acquaintance with her. And exactly what did he think he was going to ask her, anyway?

Hello, Meredith. We met at your father's wake. Any chance he or your grandfather ever mentioned Warner being haunted?

Right.

Again, he considered simply turning around and going home, but he had come this far. Besides, he knew the gnawing in his stomach wouldn't go away unless he at least tried.

As he exited his car, the door on the trailer swung open and a man stepped out onto the small wooden platform serving as a porch. The red striped boxers he was wearing contrasted with the anger on his face.

"Hey, what do you want?"

The nose and ears told him the man was a Bird. Which branch of the far-spread clan, Carl didn't know. But all of them had a reputation for both violence and balancing on the fence between legal and otherwise activities.

He used the same tone he had used cold-calling back in his early days and said, "Well, hello there, any chance Meredith is home?"

"Wha' the fuck you want to know?"

The man stumped down the two steps to the ground.

"No worries, friend," Carl still trying to project an air of friendliness and harmlessness. "Just want to talk to her." He added, "I'm not the police."

The man snorted. "Fuckin' A, you're not. Even Hopper wouldn't hire an old turd like you."

Carl didn't think Prescott Police Chief Fran Hopper would appreciate the back-handed compliment, but he had no plans to tell her. He would simply take it as a win that he was viewed as innocuous.

"So, is Meredith around?"

Glassy eyes stared back at him. Suddenly, the man turned toward the doublewide, his boxers fluttered for a moment, and Carl could see a stream of yellow hitting the Black-Eyed Susans lining a dirt strip along the trailer's edge.

This continued for an extended time, and Carl thought he had been forgotten in the other's urinary hurry. He was just going to repeat the question when the lady in question stepped out of the trailer door.

"Trav, I thought you were grabbing a toke and coming back in?"

He didn't remember her well, having simply shaken her hand and offered the standard platitudes at her father's service, but back then he would have put her in her early to mid-thirties.

The woman in front of him he would have pegged at least fifty, although she was dressed more in line with someone half her age, with cut-off shorts and a T-shirt rolled up to display an oversized pink stone hanging from her belly button. Objectively speaking, Carl thought it was a pretty stone. Unfortunately, the stomach flab hanging down over the short's waistband defeated any sense of objectivity he might have tried to attain.

"Meredith?" he called.

She turned toward the sound of his voice, finally registering there was someone other than Trav there.

"Who are you?"

"Friend of your father. We met at his wake."

Meredith squinted down at him.

"Yeah, ok." Turning to Trav, who was finishing shaking himself off and tucking things back into place. "Trav, come on, honey. I need to even things out. My shift starts in a couple of hours."

"Meredith?" Carl wondered if he was destined to repeat everything on this outing.

Her squint turned back to him. After a moment, "Yeah, lawyer friend of my fathers. So, why are you here?"

"Insurance, actually. Retired. I, ah, I wanted to talk to you. About Warner."

Something changed behind the squint.

"Don't know what you're looking for, but Warner's been dead for a long time. Nothing to talk about."

But there was. That much he could see.

"Maybe not," he said. "But I'm hoping you can help me. I think something might be happening that has to do with Warner." She continued to look at him. He added with as much emotion as he could, "Please."

Trav had finished watering the flowers and turned toward him.

"Get the fuck out of here, old man. She doesn't–"
"Wait."

Trav faced her. "Come on, Mare. It's party time, why you fuckin' around with him?"

"I know," Meredith replied, cutting him off with a wave of her hand. "The blunt should be in the glove box. Grab it."

She looked back at Carl. "What do you mean, something might be happening?"

"Someone I know was planning to go out there. He might have already."

She shrugged. "Lots do. So what?"

"I don't mean around, I mean *there*, right into town. I think he might even have decided to take a look at—"

"The shafts." Her lips barely moved as her words mimicked his own. Her already waxy face was now closer to dried plaster.

"Yes."

She slid her hand into a back pocket and pulled out a crumpled pack of cigarettes. She put one to her lips, reaching into a front pocket for a lighter.

Once it was lit, she took a deep drag and said, "Why the fuck would he do that?"

"He isn't from around here. We were talking about local history and Warner came up and–"

She cackled. "And you told him to go pay a visit? To fucking Warner? That's rich. Jesus Christ," she said, shaking her head again.

"I told him the place is dangerous. Old buildings and such." He paused. "But there's more to it than that, isn't there?"

She threw the still burning cigarette out onto the gravel. She called out to Trav, who was leaning into the sedan, searching for the joint.

He pushed. "There's something not right in Warner, is there?

Meredith snorted and pulled out another cigarette, but didn't say anything.

"What did your father tell you about Warner?"

She glanced up over her cupped hands, the lighter sputtering as it touched the tip of the Winston. "Not a damn thing. It closed down before he was born."

He felt a sense of defeat but continued, wanting to cover all the bases.

"I don't suppose he ever heard stories. Did you ever ask him?"

Spit flew out of her mouth as she blew out smoke and gave a bitter, scornful laugh. "The last time I asked my father about anything, I was twelve. The school was decorated for Christmas and I asked if we could maybe hang a few decorations up in the house, maybe even get a tree. I couldn't sit down for the next three days, including at school. Got suspended for being belligerent and never bothered going back." She shook her head. "No, mister. My father wasn't a talking kind of guy."

His deep disappointment must have touched a long dormant nerve in her because before he could thank her for her time, she added, "My grandfather did talk about it a bit before he died." She scratched her exposed stomach as she said this and studied him for a moment. "Lived with us," she said. "He was bat-shit crazy."

Rekindled hope. "Regardless, I'd appreciate anything you can tell me. It's important."

I think it is, anyway.

She continued to stare at him, then looked over toward the other car, shouting. "What the hell are you doing, Travis?"

The other man pulled back out of the sedan, a fat white paper wrapper in his hand. "Hold your fuckin' ass." He walked to the porch, taking a path right toward Carl who stood still. At the last moment, Trav changed course toward the trailer deck. He handed the joint up to Meredith, who used her cigarette to light it, tossing the Winston to the ground. She took a deep hit and held her breath for a few seconds before she blew out a wide cloud of fragrant smoke.

"Jesus, I needed that."

She focused back on him.

"What do you want to know?"

***

He considered his next steps on the drive back into town. What Meredith told him gave him nothing concrete to go on, but it had been enough to worry him even more than before his visit.

She had invited him into the trailer, and while he had not relished the thought of being in an enclosed space as she continued to work her way through the joint, he decided a contact high was a minor price to pay for any usable information.

She waved him to a ratty pea-green recliner under an open window. He settled carefully into it and leaned forward to indicate he was ready to listen, as he tried to ignore her constant itching around the large pink stone.

"He was bat-shit crazy," she had repeated, her voice raspy as she talked around the hit she was holding in. "I was a kid, but even I knew that. But," she blew out and took another hit, "he was gentle. Not like...anyways, he was gentle with me."

He sat, trying to be patient as the haze traveled slowly up and then toward him, the window unfortunately acting more a vacuum than a blower. He hoped Trav, who had peeled out saying he had to make a pickup, would not return until she shared as much as she was able or willing to share.

"I would bring him his coffee in the morning. He would be out of bed in his chair, facing the window, just looking out over the trees. He never drank it, but if I didn't bring it, he would shout, asking where it was and if I was off 'gallivanting'." She gave a wet laugh, filled with pain as all her others were, but also, he thought, affection. She coughed and put the joint down in a burned groove on the edge of the end table as she tried to catch her breath. He was wondering if the cough had set a heart attack in motion, but she finally stopped, wiping her eyes. A moment later, the joint was back in one hand as she leaned forward. His gaze kept dropping to her stomach and its adorning jewel, which had settled comfortably on the sofa cushion. She began scratching around the perimeter of the piercing again. He was glad when she spoke again and he was able to look away, back to her glassy eyes.

"Gallivanting. That's how he talked. But he used to tell me stories sometimes. Ireland, the fens, the Wee People." Her head shook as she remembered perhaps the last man who had been decent to her.

She dragged one hand across her face.

"Pops started as a hurrier when he was nine, pulling carts through the tunnels out to his mother, who finished hauling before handing it off to the breaker. His father had worked in the mines in Lancashire after leaving Ireland. Then they came here and had Pops. His father died of black lung when he was six. But you know what they say. King Coal. It was all they knew. As soon as Pops could talk the foreman into it, he switched from hurrier to miner. That was just a few weeks before the collapse."

Another suck on the quickly disappearing joint, and her fingers started again at the growing red ring around her belly button. "God damn it! I fucking *told* Trav I have sensitive skin. I should never have gotten this goddamn thing."

He was afraid he was losing her.

"Meredith. Was he there the last day? When shaft three collapsed?"

She dragged her face back toward his and nodded absently.

"He had just come off shift when they hit water. He and two other guys were the first out of the shaft. Everyone else was still below ground along with the second shift who had just come on."

"Whatever happened, it messed him up, royally. After the mine closed, he worked around, digging for the county, clearing fields for a few of the big farms, nothing steady. Until he shipped out to fight the Nazis." She snorted. "I guess being crazy wasn't a problem for that. Maybe it helped."

Quietly, and as gentle as he would be with a stray dog, he asked, "What happened when they hit water?"

"Rathcrog," she said. He shivered at the croaked word. The joint was back in her mouth, and she drew in deeply, her voice then coming out barely audible. "That was what he called it. When they hit the lake or underground river. Whatever it was."

"Rathcrog?" It tasted…wrong, and as he repeated it back, his mouth went dry.

She nodded, exhaling. "Yeah. No idea what the fuck it meant, but that was the word. There were days he would shout it, then wouldn't talk the remainder of the day. Other days, he would start yelling other shit along with it."

"Other things, like what?"

"Fire in the hole. Teeth. Bees."

A coldness washed over him.

"What?"

"I told you he was crazy," she said with a sour smile. "Christ, when he got going, he would try to get up out of his chair." Her stare was hard, but her eyes were moist. "He forgot he didn't have any *fucking legs*. How do you forget that? Jesus." She wiped her hand across her face, then took another drag. He thought he would have to prompt her again, but she started up once more.

"I would help get him back into his chair. I knew if I had to call my father, he would give Pops his medicine and he would be out until the next day. He might have been crazy, but when he was awake, I could get away with sitting in his room, which was better than the alternatives."

He hadn't wanted to ask what those alternatives were, so instead had asked,

"The shaft collapsed?" he prompted.

She nodded. "Fire in the hole. If there was a bad charge that made sense, at least. But whether someone fucked up, or it was simply a cave-in, he either didn't know or didn't say. It was blind luck he was outside the entrance when it happened. God only knows how many were trapped down there."

"And the teeth and bees?" He tried to keep his voice calm, trying to ignore the feeling of tiny little legs running up and down his entire body.

"He also told me he saw Nixon buying rubbers at Rafferty's drug store once. Didn't mean shit, except for maybe he should have been on a bigger dose of morphine."

Her eyes were wandering again, and the belly scratching had changed to a digging.

"The two people he came out with. Do you know who they were?"

"Bart Hotchkins and another guy named Lottie something. Don't know who that was."

"Hotchkins? Any relation to Pamela Hotchkins?"

She curled her lip. "What do you think?"

He knew it was a stupid question the moment he said it. While there was some influx into the area, probably over ninety percent of the current families had been in the Prescott area for generations. His own family had settled here in the mid-eighteen hundreds, changing the family name from Muller to Miller when they arrived from the Rhine area, starting out working in and, eventually, buying a general store. That lasted until the Depression when the store closed and his father had gone into insurance, starting the original incarnation of Home and Hearth Insurance.

Something else occurred to him.

"You said people might have been trapped, but I thought there were no deaths and that Forrester relocated everyone."

He jerked back at her sudden movement as she popped up and poked the half-smoked joint toward him.

"Jesus, really?" Her greasy hair swung around. "Right. Middle of the afternoon at a working mine right after a shift change and no one was hurt when the one open shaft collapses?." She stepped closer to him, and he leaned back into the chair cushion, worried that he was going to get a flicked ember in his eye. "Bullshit."

He let that hang there for a moment. "So, what happened to everyone?"

She was leaning over him now, the curtain pulled back as she scanned the front yard. He tried to pull into himself more, the crystal bouncing a few inches from the side of his face. He fought the urge to bat it away.

She muttered, "Where the fuck is he?"

He tried again, sensing his time was short.

"Meredith, is there anyone else around who had family working at the mine when it shut down?

She stepped back, the swinging stone moving away. He made himself not look at it as she sprawled on to the couch again.

"Just a few, as far as I know. Most lived in Warner itself and were working. It's not as though you could take a paid sick day. Miss Stake-up-her-ass Pamela Hotchkins. Freddie Shultz." She paused. "Lori O'Donnell. Those are the ones I can think of, anyway."

He had insured Freddie and his garage, which was still running on the eastern side of town. The O'Donnells he only knew by name and was pretty sure had moved out of state a few years back.

Less than a handful out of...how many? Had to have been dozens, at least, of miners, not counting their families.

"Then everyone else was relocated?"

She looked down at the stub in her hand, which had gone out, and popped it into her mouth.

"Weren't you listening? There was no relocation. That was some bullshit story put out by the company."

"But–"

"They fucking died! Some in the mine. The rest...I don't know."

"But their families–"

"They're dead, I said. Other than Pops, Bart, Lottie, and anyone else that managed to get out of Warner when it happened. Not many."

She stood again, and he thought she was going to rip a hole in her stomach.

"Jesus." She finally stopped digging and sat back on the tattered sofa. "What?"

She had missed his last question.

"I asked what he told you about Warner itself. And Rathcrog."

"Nothing that made sense except it scared the shit out of me."

"I—"

She snapped at him, obviously tired of the questions and probably regretting letting him in at all. "Look, there's something wrong out there. You know it, or you wouldn't be here." Her legs were twitching. "Where the hell is he?"

"Meredith?"She leaned over him again, took another look through the window, then stepped back.

"If your friend did go out there, just hope to God he didn't do anything stupid. If he has, then hope to God he's dead. For his sake and everyone else's."

She headed toward the narrow hall leading to the rear of the trailer.

"I have to get ready for work. It's wing night at the Twisted Kitty."

As she stepped through the doorway at the end of the hall, Carl called out one more question.

"How did your grandfather die?"

Meredith stopped, putting a hand up to grip the doorframe.

He could see the tendons on her hand tighten. Without turning around, she said slowly, "He burned to death. I was down at the Hill's farm, picking peas. My father was somewhere, probably getting drunk. The fire department said based on the scorch marks, they think he used the stove to light his lap blanket on fire and then just...sat there as he caught fire. They said it must have been painful as hell, but he seemed to have just...sat there. The house burned up along with him.

"Meredith, I'm–"

Click

The door closed behind her.

Stepping out of the trailer, he saw a cloud of gray following behind the approaching sedan, a manic looking Trav behind the wheel. Meredith's companion skidded to a stop just short of Carl's car and jumped out, a clear bag clenched in his fist. There was still an innate sense of danger from him, but it was now cheerful danger.

"Hey, old man, where you goin'? It's party time."

"No, thank you," he had responded. "And I believe Meredith is getting ready for work."

"Shee-it," came the reply, accompanied by a kick at the wheel well. Totally ignoring him now, Trav walked toward the trailer, calling, "Mare! Hey, Mare! Come on, darlin'! I told you I'd get it. Call in sick, why don't you. Ol' Trav needs some lovin'!"

Back in his car, he turned around in the unpaved driveway, pulled out, and headed back for Prescott.

***

He turned onto Main just a few blocks from his side street bungalow and wondered what to do now.

Dennis's house? I don't even know where he lives. I'm sure Pamela Hotchkins does, though. But what does Rathcrog mean?

An image of bees flitted through his mind, and he pushed it away, not being ready to revisit that night in high school.

It was late afternoon now, the time he would generally make his way to Tully's for the first of several whiskey and sodas, and he remembered his earlier self-promise about the double.

Besides, Dennis has office hours on Fridays, so he hasn't even gone out there yet.

When he reached the next intersection, rather than turning right toward his house, he turned left and headed for the bar.

The house smelled like a combination of feces and copper. Not that Dennis noticed. He was standing at the kitchen sink, humming a bedtime tune his mother used to sing a lifetime ago. He kept interrupting himself to run his tongue around behind his teeth. Pressure had started to build on his drive here, the initial eruptions coming as he stood at the front desk of the Prescott Inn ringing the bell.

He *tsk'd* as he looked around for a dish towel and found none. He examined the contents of each drawer and cabinet, dropping the various items onto the stained floor until he found what he was looking for hanging on the inside of the cabinet door under the sink.

Feet slipping under him, he managed to catch himself on the counter, also managing to hang onto the rather ornate carving knife in his right hand.

He wiped the nicked blade dry, as he had once carefully wiped down his dental instruments, then dropped the now red-stained towel alongside an egg slicer on the linoleum floor.

"Enns?"

The slurred voice came from the bedroom, just off the kitchen.

He stepped to the open doorway and looked down at the naked form curled up on the bed like a small child taking a nap.

"Enns, peez."

A hand reached toward him in supplication. Shallow swirls and designs were etched on the back of the hand and extended up the arm to the shoulder. The other arm had similar slender lines, not matching but somehow complementing the others. The face was unmarked, but a dried smear covered the lower lip and chin.

"Peez."

He stood admiring his work, tongue running around inside his mouth. He felt a sharp prick and a drop of blood seeped down his throat.

The hum in his head, his constant companion, buzzed more excitedly, but there was a note of caution as well.

He had the image of lock tumblers slowly lining up as the whining voice continued.

"Enns, peez!"

The outstretched hand vibrated with the intensity of the emotions behind the muttering.

Well, I do deserve a break. It's been a long, productive day. And more work to do tonight.

He dropped the knife blade down, and its thin sharp edge sank into the bare wood floor. He reached his own hand out and squeezed the other, then pulled back and dropped his stained and crusted pants.

The woman, formerly known as Pamela Hotchkins, smiled. As he swung a leg up and over, her mouth opened, the remaining stub of her tongue bouncing as she squealed in delight.

Chapter 4

Carl had the thought that everything went in cycles, as he looked around the packed parking lot. Even bar crowds. In his youth, Fridays were the big night out for most, with freshly cashed paychecks in hand. Saturdays were for sobering up before Sunday sermons. He wasn't sure when the over-indulging day changed to Saturdays. As he pulled open the door to the bar, he wondered if it had anything to do with the decline of churchgoing. Not that he was one to criticize. Pat Larkin's funeral was the last time he had entered the First Centenary Church of Prescott; before that, when his wife was laid to rest.

Nodding to several acquaintances and former customers, he looked around for an open table but wasn't surprised that none appeared available.

He normally preferred to sit at the bar, which gave him both a good vantage of any excitement that broke out and a good chance of striking up a conversation. Always gregarious, he had become more so since Regina's death.

Today, however, he had hoped to have a quiet spot to try to work through things. Barring that, he looked around the horseshoe bar. There was a single open stool second from one curved end, wedged between a large middle-aged man he didn't know and a young woman who looked somewhat familiar. Probably the daughter, now grown, of an old client. He would take it.

Squeezing and muttering 'sorry' to each as he pulled the stool out and slid onto it, he raised two fingers to catch Leo's eye. The bartender saw the motion, nodded, and motioned back with his own finger to show he would be over shortly.

He leaned forward on the bar, content to wait until his drink arrived as he tried to get a handle on the day's events.

He was feeling a bit claustrophobic by the time the glass was put in front of him. The large man on his left kept gesturing as he spoke to a companion on the gesturer's other side, arms swinging and coming perilously close to hitting him each time. While the woman on his right was slight, Carl was aware of her proximity at all times. Like human dominoes, each time the large hairy arm almost hit him, he leaned back. After the third time, he turned to the woman and dipped his head in an unspoken apology. She accepted it as silently and tried to scoot her stool another half inch toward the turn of the bar.

Mr. Gesture got up to leave and, before another in the hovering crowd could fill the seat, Carl scooted over.

Turning again to his right, he said, "Quick, put your purse on it," gesturing to his former perch. "Pretend you're with someone."

The young woman looked startled, then pulled up a backpack from the floor next to her and plopped it onto the seat.

"Good idea," she nodded, mouth quirking, then added, "Thanks," before turning back toward the open room.

"You Ida's granddaughter? Ida Brackston?"

A song had started on the jukebox, and he raised his voice to be heard over it. The woman turned back to him with a considering look. "No. She was my aunt. Technically great-aunt," she amended. "Do I know you?"

He nodded with satisfaction. "No, but I knew Ida. Your smirk reminded me of her."

The laugh was genuine and lighthearted and, if there were a scale for such expressions, it would have been on the opposite end from Meredith's earlier ones. He found himself chuckling along with her.

"I was warned when I moved here." She held out her hand. "Holly Wilmingham."

He grasped the hand with his own. "Carl Miller. You didn't grow up in Prescott?" He knew she hadn't, but the first few sips of his double were just starting to dissipate the edges of his worries. Time enough to decide what to do next. For the moment, working his way through a couple of cocktails and chatting with a pretty young woman was just what the doctor ordered.

She shook her head, and he noticed a faded pink streak running down the side of her auburn shoulder length hair. "Morgantown. Mom stayed there after graduating from M.U., met Dad, and then I came into the picture. I moved here a couple of months ago for work." She said it in a practiced way, and he was certain she had to answer the question multiple times a day. Then she smiled again, and he wondered at the lack of admirers. Although Tully's demographics tended to slant older, the Twisted Kitty catering more to the younger set, there were still a fair number of twenty and thirty somethings around the bar.

Unbidden, a vision of a dangling pink stone came to mind, and he shook it away.

"What do you do for work?" he asked.

"I'm a cop."

Well, that would explain it. Folks still trying to get a handle on her and playing it safe.

"For Frannie, then."

A slight look of shock.

"Frannie? You mean Chief Hopper?"

It was his turn to laugh.

"Yes, Chief Hopper. Sorry, I've known her since she was in diapers. Old habits."

The idea that the Chief of Police had ever been anything *but* the Chief, let alone in diapers, seemed not to be something that had ever occurred to the woman.

"Um...ok. But yeah, I'm the overnight dispatcher." There was a note of disappointment in her voice but then she added hopefully, "The Chief did tell me as soon as an opening for patrol comes up, I'm first on her list, though.

He didn't have the heart to tell her that the last new patrol officer had been appointed nine years before, after Hector Gross keeled over from a heart attack. Gross was sixty-eight at the time and had been on the force for thirty-seven years.

He made an agreeable sound and said, "Didn't realize they had an overnight dispatcher."

"They didn't until I was hired. Guess things have gotten busier in Prescott."

Guess Frannie had extra money in her budget and didn't want to lose it.

"I imagine so. Why aren't you working tonight?"

"Even dispatchers get days, or nights, off. Callie, the daytime dispatcher, is taking forwarded calls at home tonight. I do the same for her in reverse."

At his nod of understanding she said, "You said you knew Aunt Ida?"

"Yep, I was in school with her. Your grandmother was a few years behind us." His eyes twinkled as he teased, "If you're looking for any juicy stories, you're out of luck. Ida was always the good girl in school. Prim and proper through and through."

He enjoyed seeing her laugh. "Damn. And here I thought I might finally get her down off that family pedestal."

He smiled and took another sip, enjoying the warmth of both the whiskey and the banter, as Meredith and Warner slipped to a back corner of his mind. The dispatcher's cell phone, sitting on the bar, started vibrating. She picked it up, spoke briefly and, mouthing an apology his way, stood and walked out the door.

He was pushing the melting ice cubes in his now empty glass when she came back. The smile was gone.

"He's an ass," he said.

She looked at him. "She. But how did you know?"

He managed to limit his surprise to raised eyebrows, reminding himself that the twenty-first century had reached even Prescott, and held his glass aloft at her correction. "I'm old. And I saw that look often enough in the mirror a millennium or two ago. I've probably caused a few of them, although I'd like to think I wasn't as big a jerk as most are at your age."

That, at least, garnered a crinkle of her eyes.

"She didn't get out until late tonight," she said, apologizing for the unseen woman. "And with the two-hour drive from Morgantown, she–"

"Oh, I'm sure," he said, waving away her explanation. "She's still an ass. But her assiness is my gain." He waved at Leo, indicating to refill Holly's almost empty wine glass along with his own spent tumbler. "At my age, anyone willing to talk, and not about some celebrity I've never heard of, is a godsend."

This time it was more a smirk than smile and he saw a teenage Ida's face overlaid on Holly's. It wasn't the time to mention it, but he had dated Ida before she had broken up with him following him exhibiting some of that aforementioned jerkiness that seemed to afflict all teenage boys.

"So, you've always wanted to be a cop, drove your parents crazy when you were young, wanted toy guns instead of Barbies, and were a black belt by the time you were twelve. Do I have that right?"

She had just raised her refreshed drink to her lips and sputtered a bit, causing the Merlot to splash onto the polished bar.

"Stop that!" Her tone turned mock insulted. "And no." She raised her nose as she spoke, but the crinkles were still there. "I had a Barbie plus guns. And I didn't get my black belt until I was sixteen, Mr. Know-it-All."

"My mistake," he replied, toasting her correction.

She turned the questions back to him.

"What brings you to Tully's tonight? Is this your standard watering hole?" She grinned. "The Twisted Kitty not your cup of tea?"

He shook his head, grinning in return. "Obviously not yours either. I prefer a place where I can actually have a conversation without shouting constantly." He made a face as the jukebox kicked back on and continued in a louder voice. "I stand corrected. As for what brings me here…Well, I was visiting out at Banyon Lake today and needed a good alcohol swab afterwards." He downed the last of his drink. "Internal, external, they both work."

She said, "Banyon Lake?" A squint. "South of here, right?" At his nod, she said. "Technically, it's in our jurisdiction, but I haven't taken any calls from there yet."

He replied with a straight face, "Well, it isn't the hotbed of crime that Prescott is, certainly."

With a chuckle, she poked his arm.

"What were you doing out there?"

He hesitated.

"Oops," she said. "Sorry. None of my business. Just making conversation." She said it as an apology. "It really wasn't my cop showing. Remember, I'm just a dispatcher."

"No apology necessary." Paused again, then said, more seriously, "Just trying to scratch a very old itch".

"It doesn't have to do with Warner, does it?"

He looked at her.

Looking embarrassed, she said, "I'm a history buff. When I took the dispatcher job, I started reading about Prescott and came across a reference to Warner." A frown. "I tried googling it, but came up blank, which I found strange, since the little I had read seemed to show Prescott and Warner were tied at the hip."

He studied her a moment longer.

"Yes, it does," he said, finally. "And I've been trying to figure something out. Maybe a second set of eyes would help..."

Holly checked her phone once more before climbing into bed, both hoping and dreading a text from Lauren. She had known it would be difficult to maintain a long-distance relationship when she made the move to Prescott but had been willing to put in the effort. Apparently, she was the only one. Tonight wasn't the first time Lauren had blown off coming to see her, and even when she visited Morgantown, her girlfriend's enthusiasm seemed forced.

Ah well, it's not like I was in love with her, anyway. Was I?

That was a conversation with herself for another time. Right now, she was 'wired and tired' as her father always said when she was stomping her feet at bedtime, insisting she wasn't ready to go to bed.

There was a mewing from under the bed and she leaned over to see the stray she had taken in a few weeks before and creatively named Mr. Whiskers, limp out onto the throw rug. When he showed up prowling around the old house where she had her second-story apartment, his paw had been missing fur and showed signs he'd had a run-in with another stray. But he had taken to her right away, put up with the cleaning and bandaging, and condescended to sleep in her bedroom, rotating between under it when she wasn't home and on top when she was.

She lifted him up and set him beside her. His purring paused briefly during the journey, then started back up as she continued her musings.

Carl was an odd duck, but she liked him. He reminded her a bit of her grandfather, although Gramps had been a teetotaler and Carl could probably drink her under the table. That was why, after a lot of chatting and his fifth drink, she had insisted on driving him home. He balked, but finally agreed when she promised to pick him up in the morning to get his car.

But what he had told her? It sounded more like something out of a horror movie than the real world. Haunted town? Rag...whatever that word was that he mentioned.

Still, it was odd she hadn't been able to find anything online about Warner. And Carl said no one really talked about it, except to mention Prescott was an offshoot before the mining company shut down.

I wonder if the Chief knows anything.

She decided she would ask the next time she saw her. Chief Hopper was often still in the office when Holly started her shift. She was a bit intimidated by the Chief but knew that was her own issue. Chief Hopper had always been very friendly, in a professional way.

She set her phone down on the nightstand, pulled the covers up, and turned out the light. But her mind wouldn't turn off. She was still awake an hour later mulling things over, when her phone chirped an incoming text message.

He looked even older than her guess of eighty or so in the yellow porch light, his baggy pajamas fluttering.

"Holly? Rather early to get my car, isn't it?" Blue eyes blinked owlishly at her.

"Carl, a report came in about a fire out at Banyon Lake."

His eyes cleared.

"Where?"

"The property belongs to a Meredith Baxter. That's the woman you went to see today, right?"

He motioned for her to come in, nodding, and said, "Give me just a minute to pull some pants on." The baggie pajamas disappeared around a doorway, followed by the sound of drawers opening and closing.

She looked around, noticing the flowered curtains and butterfly-themed knick-knacks. He had told her he was a widower, so she assumed these were leftovers from his wife's decorating. She also noticed a fair covering of dust on all the horizontal surfaces in sight.

He was back in less than five minutes, albeit with a slight list to his step.

"Right," he said. "Let's go."

Driving toward the outskirts of town, she looked at the dash clock.

Christ, was it just a couple of hours ago?

She focused on the unlit, winding road, still not comfortable with what locals referred to as 'country driving'.

"What?" Carl had said something she didn't quite catch. She glanced at him, not wanting to take her eyes off the road for long. He was staring out his window, hand holding tight to the grab bar above the door.

"Rathcrog. What does it mean?"

She had no answer.

Ten minutes later, as she turned her Jeep down the same gravel drive Carl had traveled that afternoon, she could smell smoke and see an orange glow ahead through the trees.

Flashing red and blue lights added to the almost party-like view as she pulled up behind a Prescott police car. Both town fire trucks were parked on what passed for the front lawn. The rumble of their engines, powering the truck's onboard water tanks, provided background bass to the hissing of the hoses spraying the conflagration.

"Hey, Holly. What are you doing out here?"

Larry Welkins, one of the five night shift patrol officers, was standing off to one side, watching the firefighters do what they could to save the metal structure, but looking at the buckling walls she could tell it was a lost cause.

She gestured over to Carl, who had exited the car as well and was staring at the blaze. "I saw the department text spray and thought he might have some information that could be helpful."

Larry looked over at Carl, whose bit of remaining hair whipped around from the fire's blow-back.

Larry nodded, although it was obvious he found her statement suspect. "The Chief is around back." His partner, Fred, stepped out from their patrol car and said they were clear to return to the station. Another nod, this one in Fred's direction, and Larry said, "Catch you later, Holly."

She gave a chopping wave and walked over to Carl.

"Hey, I want to go talk to Chief." When he didn't respond immediately, she touched his shoulder.

He jerked as though slapped. From the look on his face, she doubted he had registered she was there.

"What? Of course. Yes, of course."

He shuffled along beside her, carefully stepping over the hose as the Prescott firefighters continued their doomed fight against the blaze.

The Chief was talking to Fire Chief Gamble as they approached.

"—doubt it, but it looks like at least... Holly? What are you doing out here?"

She felt her cheeks burn and fought the urge to snap to attention.

"Hi Chief. I heard about the fire and, well, thought you might be able to use extra help." She knew how lame it sounded and added, "Also, Carl here might know something that might help."

The woman, over half a foot taller than Holly's five-three, looked between Holly and Carl for a moment as Gamble excused himself and walked back toward the front of the trailer.

Carl said, "Hi, Frannie."

She winced at the casualness of Carl's greeting, but the Chief simply dipped her head and said, "Howdy, Carl. You know something about what happened here?"

Carl shook his head but said, "I was out here earlier today, talking to Meredith."

Dark eyebrows shot up. "Why?"

"I was, ah, interested in comparing notes on some local history I thought she might know something about."

If the Chief's eyebrows went up any higher, she thought they were going to meet her hairline.

"Uh, huh," Chief Hopper said. "You drove out to talk history with Meredith Baxter."

Carl looked uncomfortable but replied, "Well, she did grow up around here."

A derisive snort. "Along with everyone else." A brief glance her way. "With a few exceptions."

Carl said nothing.

"Any idea where she might be?"

He shook his head. "No, she was here when I left, along with Travis Bird."

"Travis Bird? Shee-it, I hadn't heard he was out of County." Hopper ran her hand through her cropped hair and looked back toward the flames that were now just a few feet off the ground. The metal walls of the trailer were now buckled and had collapsed onto themselves.

"Drug deal gone bad?" Holly was startled at the question but then realized it was rhetorical as the Chief mused possibilities staring into the fire.

"No," the older woman answered herself. "Doesn't feel right. Well, we'll add him to the list of persons of interest." She used her shoulder radio and asked Callie to add a 'BOLO', cop short-hand for 'Be on the lookout', for Travis Bird, sometimes known as Travis Clements, also T-Bird, to the one already issued for Meredith Baxter. Hopper had turned back to Carl to say something, but a shout interrupted her.

"Chief Hopper!" The fire chief was calling from the front.

Hopper led as the three walked back to him.

She could make out Gambles' flickering, pale image past her car a few yards into the wood line. He was standing, looking down at the ground. There was a firefighter bent over nearby.

When they stepped up to stand next to him, she realized his paleness wasn't a trick of the firelight. His face was colorless. As she looked down into the creeping vines, her own face drained and her stomach gave a lurch.

The general shape was something she had seen innumerable times at county fairs and block parties, where everyone chipped in toward the barbeque. But the haunch that lay in the kudzu was nothing that had ever hung in a butcher shop, at least outside the darkest nightmare. Covered with short, slightly curled hairs, the pale flesh faded to bright red and splintered white bone at either end. A puckered scar ran about an inch up its length.

Next to her, Carl let out a moan.

Chief Hopper said quietly, "Well, now."

There was a retching sound from the helmeted firefighter who straightened up after a moment, then wiped his coat sleeve across his mouth.

"You ok, Max?" Gambles asked.

Watery red eyes looked back, and the firefighter nodded. He made the mistake of letting his gaze drop again, and he swallowed another heave.

Voice gentle, the fire chief said, "Go around and see if Paul and Sherry need any help."

The firefighter nodded again. Fist up against his mouth, he quickly departed.

Gambles turned to face Chief Hopper.

"We should have this about red up in another hour." When it came to colloquialisms, even Morgantown was local, and Holly knew he meant cleaned up.

He pointed at the hacked flesh with the toe of his boot. "I'll leave this to you." He started down the same path Max had followed. Part way down it, she heard him say, "And thank God for that."

She fought a continuing urge to gag but refused to with the Chief standing right next to her.

"Holly?"

"Yes, Ma'am."

There was a hesitation, and she wondered if she was about to be chastised for her formality, a regular occurrence when she spoke with Chief Hopper. But damn it, this was a formal situation. If a severed partial human leg wasn't, what was?

But Hopper tone was mild. "Get Marshall out here. And get hold of Callie and cancel that BOLO on Travis Bird."

"Ma'am?"

"I somehow don't think he's hobbling around without the top part of his leg."

The gorge started back up her throat.

"That's his leg?" she asked.

Hopper pointed. "Well, unless someone else in the county has a scar that matches the one he got wrestling with me a couple of years ago at the Kitty, I'd say yep." The Chief turned and gave a small smile. "Mine is smaller, but scars tend to happen when a broken beer bottle is involved in a drunk and disorderly arrest.

She knew the Birds by reputation only, but from all descriptions they leaned toward the super-sized, violent, and dumb side of the homo sapiens scale. She looked at the other woman again with a bit of awe. Nodding at the directive, she headed back to her car. As she was off duty, she didn't have her personal radio, but there was one mounted on her dash. She heard Carl speaking to her boss as she ducked into her car to make the call to Callie, switching channels for a direct connection to headquarters. Besides canceling the BOLO on Bird, she asked for the County Coroner, Marshall Lovell, to be dispatched.

"It happen in the fire?" Callie's young sounding voice came through, sounding tired and slightly bored.

Hesitating, she finally answered. "Homicide. And Callie, we'll need a full scene kit too."

"Jesus, Holly. Homicide?" There was excitement in the voice now. Murder wasn't unknown in Prescott or its vicinity but was still rare. The last one had been a botched convenient store robbery about four years before. "Bird?"

"Yeah," she replied. Then, "Callie, you grew up here, right? What do you know about Warner?"

She could sense the puzzlement on the other end.

"Warner? Just that it's been empty about a hundred years." A giggle followed this statement. "I spent a night out there back in high school. Trevor Howard, he was a senior and the team quarterback, and I was just a sophomore. He convinced me to go look at the stars with him. We–"

She cut off the other dispatcher's reminiscing. "I mean, what do you know about the town itself? And you spent the night out there. In Warner itself?"

"Well, no, of course not. Too dangerous. We were a-ways back in the woods. But I could see the tops of a few buildings before it got too dark. As for Warner itself, like I said, it's just a bunch of old buildings. The mine got tapped out or something. Why? Does the fire have something to do with Warner?"

"Thanks, Callie," Holly said and ended the call.

She found Carl and the Chief at a weathered picnic table upwind from the smoldering trailer remains and quietly took a seat next to Carl as her boss paced back and forth in front of the table. Looking at Carl in confusion, she was about to ask him what was going on when Chief Hopper spoke.

"A haunted town? Are you freaking kidding me?" There was disbelief on Hopper's face and in her tone.

Ah, he told her.

"I know what it sounds like, Frannie. And I didn't say it was haunted. Just that there seems to be something about Warner that might be related to what's going on. But considering the circumstances and timing, I—"

"Don't bull me, Carl. Disclaimers aside, that's exactly what you're saying." Carl seemed to be chewing a hole into his cheek as she continued. "I don't buy it. I was born here, and I've heard the same stories you have. Hell, I spent a couple of nights graduation week out in Warner."

"In or nearby?"

The uniformed woman looked at him.

"I'll take that as an answer. It's almost as though most people have a built-in defense mechanism, avoiding Warner itself. I don't–"

"Like a mouse avoiding a snake hole." The words came out of her mouth without thought and both Carl and the Chief turned to face her.

Her stomach dropped at the glare she received, but she held her gaze until Chief Hopper looked at the old man again.

"It's just it's too dangerous out there. I was always told–"

Carl interjected, "Of course. We were all told that. But, forgive me, Frannie, we were teenagers. By definition, built to ignore what we were told by our parents. So why didn't you at least go into the town and explore?"

The Chief had a thoughtful frown. She said, "I...don't know," and sat down, much too close to her for comfort.

Her discomfort increased when the Chief casually reached out and put a hand on her shoulder in commiseration of the situation. Thankfully, a voice crackling through Hopper's radio broke the moment. It was Callie canceling the BOLO on Travis Bird.

"Frannie, what happens now?" Carl gestured around at the charred trailer. The flames toward the front were dying down as the blaze ran out of fuel. The firefighters were working on dousing the remnants.

"Once Granger and his folks get things settled—"

"No," he interjected, "I mean about...the rest."

"Nothing," came the short reply, and Hopper gave him a steady look. "We'll keep looking for Meredith and I'm going to add Dennis Tierney to the look out to see what, if anything, he knows about this," she waved her hand toward the trailer's charred remains, "as well as have someone swing by Pamela Hotchkins's in case he's with her."

"But–"

"I appreciate you coming out here and letting me know about Tierney's planned trip. But," she looked at Holly, "that's it. Nothing more. There isn't anything else. Some meth head went over the edge and set fire to her own house, most likely." She turned and began walking back toward the parking area. "Shit like this happens. Too often."

A few seconds later, Carl said, "Holly, we have to–"

"Nothing, Carl." The Chief had spoken, so that was that. "You told the Chief what you think, or believe, and she made her decision."

So why couldn't she hold his eyes?

Thank God Trav had made it back as the old man was leaving. After the dried-up fuck's visit, Meredith didn't know if she could work her shift at the Kitty straight.

She finished drying off and dropped the towel next to the shower stall. Trav's snoring came through the door, his breathing pausing after each exhale as his body decided moment to moment if it should even bother.

She was on the downside and knew she would need a 'perk up' during her break tonight.

Since she left her father's house at sixteen, she had avoided thinking about her grandfather, and everything else, from her childhood.

Fucking old fuck.

She didn't know why she had agreed to talk to him and more than regretted it now, as long-stashed memories refused to go back in a mental lockbox.

One in particular kept poking at her. She had told the old man the truth, that she was picking peas the day Pops set fire to the house and himself. But she hadn't told him about earlier that day, before she left to earn the two dollars she needed for her hidden stash.

The morning had started as usual. Drunken snores from her father, scattered empty bottles of Pabst littering the scarred coffee table and floor around the sofa where he lay semi-comatose. She had brewed a pot of coffee and, being as quiet as she could, brought it down the hall to Pops' room. He had already managed to pull himself from his bed into the wheelchair, a feat that had become somewhat sporadic over the previous few months. Rather than rolling to the window closest to his bed as he normally did, he was sitting facing the other window. That view ended half a dozen yards away at the tree line. The forest behind it extended most of a mile before the old growth changed to shrubs that had grown up around the periphery of Warner since its abandonment.

She put the coffee mug on the nightstand and carried the table to set it next to him. He didn't speak, but continued the low humming she sometimes heard him make. She hoped it wouldn't be one of his bad days and that she wouldn't have to wake her father to help handle him. Even at his worst, she preferred to be with Pops rather than deal with the hands and, sometimes, fists, of the man that helped create her and was of a mind to 'keep it in the family', as the saying went.

She sat on the side of his bed, enjoying the silence, and mentally counted for the hundredth time how much she had in the tin can in the back of her closet, then how much the pea picking would add to it today. She was still short twelve dollars, even after a year of working and scrimping, before she could pay the first two months at the Prescott Arms rooming house.

Pops' humming rose from an undertone and the old man began rhythmically hitting the arm of his wheelchair with his left hand.

'Shit,' she had thought.

'Molly! Lock the door, Molly!'

Molly had been her grandmother's name.

"Dead, all dead! Rathcrog!"

That word.

When he first came out with it, she assumed she misheard the gargled sound. But after hearing him intermittently shout it out for a few weeks, she had asked the assistant school librarian on the off chance it was Irish. Mrs. Callahan had emigrated from Cork with her husband a few years before, her man landing a job working at the glass foundry, she at the junior high. The woman had always been kind to her, feeding her love of books by suggesting various titles and skipping the fines for any books her father had found and destroyed.

"Where did you hear that word, Meredith?"

"My Pops." she had said. "He isn't right in the head, but he's been saying it a lot lately. Since he's from Ireland and I know you are, I thought–"

"It's not something for a little girl to worry about, dear." The woman had looked…spooked, was the word that came to mind.

Like one of those people on the movie posters outside the Prescott Rialto when they were advertising a horror movie.

She had frowned but wasn't willing to give up on it. She thought that, maybe, if she knew what it meant, she could help Pops. At least understand why he got so upset when he said it. She loved him, even more than the stray cat she had taken in and let sleep with her, until he disappeared one day after her father came home following r a particularly bad bender and she found him passed out with scratches on his hands and dark red stains on his undershirt.

Mrs. Callahan had looked at her before finally replying. "It means Hell's Gate. It's just a story from the Old Country, passed down to keep children in line. That's it."

"But–"

"I said that's it, Meredith." Then gently, "Now, I put aside 'Black Beauty' for you. I know how much you love animals and..."

Hearing her grandfather shout once again, she had gone to Pops and squatted down next to his chair. She took his hand in her own and said, "It's ok, Pops. Everything is ok. You're safe. Everyone is safe. And I'm here."

She gave the hand a gentle squeeze.

He had whipped his head toward her, his fingers digging into her palm.

"No, it's still there. Waiting. We sealed it in, but it's still there. Should have blown the whole goddamn town. Don't–"

"Shhh, Pops. It's ok."

He had jerked his hand from hers. She pulled back, shocked, and looked at him. There was a light in his eyes. Coherency, she realized. He was totally there, at least at the moment.

"Goddamn it, girl. We blew the shaft, but it was too late. So many...". The light hadn't faded, but tears superimposed it. "All dead. But it isn't. I don't know that it can die. It's looking for a way out. I can hear it."

Before she could reply, the light blinked out, and he started humming again, staring out at the trees.

She checked herself in the mirror. Her work blouse was passable clean, her name in large print on the plastic tag under the slightly smaller words 'Twisted Kitty'.

After running a brush through her hair, she decided she was as ready as she would be and went back into the bedroom. Trav continued his intermittent snores, and she reached into the jeans crumpled on the floor. The plastic bag she pulled out went into her own pocket.

Thump, Thump.

It better not be the old fuck, again.

She pushed open the door. A man, disheveled but with a close-lipped smile stood just to the side.

"Hi Meredith."

She opened her mouth to tell him to get the hell off her property when his lips parted in a wide grin. A warm stream ran down her leg.

She tried to close the door, but her body refused to obey.

He stepped forward, a jug in one hand, and patted her shoulder with the other.

"It's all good. You've been Chosen."

***

Travis Bird sat up, shrieking at the first blow, staring without recognition at the two people on either side of the bed. He looked down at the raw, gaping wound that extended halfway through his thigh just above the knee, the bone still tenuously connected but splintered to reveal yellowish-red marrow. He screamed again as he tried to roll to the side.

Bone was harder to cut through than he would have thought, Dennis mused. He nodded at the woman on the other side of the bed, and she grabbed Travis's shoulders, pinning him back. The cleaver rose and came down again, harder this time.

Following the successful second attempt, the axe swung back and whipped through the air horizontally, the woman stepping out of its path just in time. Travis's head sat on top of the wide blade for a moment, mouth open for another scream, then tumbled into the corpse's lap.

The brief geyser of blood quickly settled to a *glurping*, making its way down the body in a slow sheet.

A shame he has so many tattoos and scars, Tierney thought, but we should be able to salvage at least part of it. Every little bit helps.

He nodded again at the woman, designated the Stríocálaí, the Worker, by the power of the Source. She limped to the kitchen area, blood droplets following her red-soaked, formerly white sneakers and began rustling through the under-sink cupboard. As she did, he turned his attention back to the body, contemplating where to start. The skinning was to be done elsewhere, but he would prefer not to have to transport an intact body.

Two more blows and the marred thigh was free.

He pushed it off the bed with the blade and began chopping again to make more manageable pieces.

The trailer's owner returned holding multiple plastic garbage bags and a can of lighter fluid.

He paused in his efforts and told her to start filling the bags.

"And no gallivanting, young lady."

She nodded happily.

Chapter 5

Dennis didn't pay attention to the scrunching up of the
check-out girl's face nor her slight gag as she scanned the jugs of
water any more than he had noticed Mark Turner's look when
he checked out at the hardware store. He wheeled the grocery
cart to his car and proceeded to open and dump the contents
of the one-gallon jugs on the ground next to it. He ignored
the water sloshing over his scuffed boots, although enough had
seeped in that they made a squishing noise as he deposited the
now empty containers in the back seat. His tongue ran around
in his mouth, dipping as it passed multiple gaps, then pushed
against two molars on one side. There was a smaller version of
the sounds his boots made as he did. His dirt and blood grimed
fingers reached into the back of his mouth.

Pop!

One then the other came loose, their roots coming free as
well. He spit them into his hand and examined the small shreds
of red tissue clinging to the roots, then popped the teeth back
into his mouth, sucking and rolling them around. They made a

slight clicking sound as they bounced against the new growths lining the inside of the original tooth line. He swallowed the hanging flesh that was buffed from the dislodged teeth and, finally, downed the teeth themselves.

One of his patients walking across the parking lot waved as he pulled out onto the road, but he ignored them. He also ignored the rustling in the back seat. The ride was silent except for intermittent low sounds from the back of the SUV.

He pulled off the county road onto what had once been the principal thoroughfare leading into Warner and turned to the passenger seat.

"There's a collapsible wagon behind the seats. Put the bags and equipment into it, then load the jugs." He motioned toward the back seat. "Bring that with you as well."

Meredith Baxter, now *Stríocálaí*, looked slightly disheveled but, except for a bloody pattern on one cheek that looked like it had been gouged out, not much different from when Carl had paid a visit. She turned from where she had been staring out the windshield and nodded toward him with absent eyes, then got out and went around to open the hatch.

She pulled the cart around and began tossing the jugs into it. When the last one was loaded, there was shuffling from the back seat and the husk of Pamela Hotchkins, Source-named the *Fuilier*, or *Blood*, stood beside her.

They both stepped up to the driver's window.

He had expected to go with them back to Warner, but a whispering thrum corrected that.

"Follow the trail into town. You'll know where to go from there. I need to take care of something in Prescott. I'll meet you a bit later." He reached out and dug the tip of his finger into the wound in Meredith's cheek. She gave a small gasp as he did. The husk made a low keening.

"Not now," he said as he licked his finger, then pulled away.

He wasn't certain where Carl Miller lived, but wasn't worried. He knew he would find it.

***

Carl had tried to talk to Holly on the drive back, but received only terse head shakes in return, so he had given up and remained silent the rest of the way to his house.

And he was tired. So tired. He wanted to crawl into bed, or a glass of whiskey, and not come out for a few days.

He thanked the dispatcher as he got out of her car and Holly gave a slight head dip, but still didn't speak.

Inside, he took off his overcoat and made his way to the kitchen. Events definitely called for a night-cap.

He heard the chime of his old-fashioned doorbell. *Did she change her mind?*

He called out, "Hang on!" as he splashed two fingers of whiskey on top of the single cube in his glass.

When he opened the door, he was greeted by a spectre. It looked like Dennis Tierney, but the figure standing at the door was filthy, dried mud and mottled, darker stains splattered across his face, exposed hands, and torn clothing.

And the eyes. They seemed to look through, or inside, him and whatever was behind them, it wasn't the man he had shared cocktails and small talk with.

"Dennis, are you all right? People, the police, are looking for you."

The figure stepped across the threshold. As the dentist closed the few feet between them, a stench hit Carl that caused him to step back. He was hit again, this time with a scent-memory. It had been a youthful hunting trip, and he had come across an animal carcass at the edge of a pond, half eaten by scavengers and long decaying.

"Dennis?" He repeated in a croak, mouth suddenly dry.

His testicles tried to crawl up inside his body as the man who had been Dennis Tierney focused on him. The corners of the mouth pulled up in a mocking mimicry of a smile. Pooled blood surrounded multiple gaps in the mouth and sharp points and serrated edges of new growth, like the baby teeth of a deep-sea predator, showed behind the holes.

A hand reached out and grasped his shoulder, fingers digging in harshly to his flesh, grinding the bone in its socket. He saw the other hand pull back in a fist before it crashed into his face.

Holly thought she had remained awake, but her eyes opened and when she grabbed her cell off the bedside table out of habit, saw she had missed a text message. She sat up, Mr. Whiskers protesting the disturbance.

She felt an internal tug, wondering if it was a message from Lauren, but realized she didn't really care if it was.

Too little, too late.

There were two messages, both station sprays. The first was the updated BOLO Chief Hopper had said would be going out regarding Dennis Tierney. The second was one for Pamela Hotchkins.

She stared at that one for a moment and then scrolled through her contacts for Burt Lowell.

He picked up after the second ring.

"Isn't it your night off?"

"Yeah, but I've been monitoring the messages. A lot of excitement tonight."

"No shit," he said. "Total cluster. I take it you know about the fire out at Banyon Lake?"

"I actually took a drive out to the Baxter place. Total loss."

"That's what I heard," he replied. "So, what's up? Finally decided to change teams?" It was half teasing, half hopeful. He was more than a bit of an asshole, but being one of only three cops, plus her, that normally worked the night shift, they had established a sort of verbally armed, semi-friendly truce.

"You wish," she said. "What's the latest? I saw the notice for Hotchkins and Tierney."

She heard him blow out a breath before he continued in a slightly confused voice, in contrast to his usual tone. "Fucked if I know. The Chief asked me to check his place and if he wasn't there, go talk to her. He wasn't around, and neither was she, but..."

"Go on."

"Her kitchen. When I got there, there were pools of what looked like blood on the floor."

"You didn't just go in, did you?" She was appalled at the thought, having sat through numerous lectures at the Academy about probable cause.

"Fuck, Holly," came back the insulted reply. "Of course not. I saw it through the back door and called it in to Hopper. She said it was enough to enter, so I did. And it was blood. But the kitchen wasn't the biggest thing..."

He left her hanging, and she cursed him in her mind.

"Burt," she forced the next word out. "Please."

She knew he was smiling, damn him.

"Very polite, Officer Wilmingham. Just past the kitchen, there was a bedroom. Streaks and drips running from the kitchen back to it. The bed, though, that was the coop-dee-graw."

"I don't think that word means what you think it means," she replied. "But give. What about the bedroom?"

"Blame Stuart Junior College. Look…it was a goddamn meat locker," he said, his voice flat. "The puddles leading to it were just a warm-up for the bed itself. It looked like someone had butchered a pig on it."

"Blood?" she asked, her body going numb.

He snorted so loudly she pulled the phone away from her ear for a moment. "Either that or someone was filming a remake of Halloween. Yeah, it was blood. Smeared on the walls, too, like someone had tried to draw a picture on one of them, right next to the bed."

"A picture of what?" She remembered her snubbing of Carl on the drive back. "Cut the shit, Burt."

"I don't know," he replied. Before she could contradict him, he added earnestly, "Really, I don't, Holly. It was sort of rectangular shaped, but that's all I could say. There were squiggles in the middle of it, like a psychotic kindergartener had tried to write a note."

A slight pause, then, "Maybe Hotchkins was using." It was more question than statement, with a touch of both hope and fear in it.

It was the hint of the latter that rattled her. Sarcasm, inappropriate joking, racist comments, all were part and parcel of Burt's personae. She guessed it was, partly, a shield, but if so, what he had seen at Hotchkins' house now caused it to slip.

She fought an urge to say something reassuring, knowing how it would be received, and focused on the last comment. In Prescott County, *using* was another way of saying *on meth*. Meredith Baxter and Travis Bird were far from the only ones using in the depressed area. But it didn't hang together for her any more than it had for Chief Hopper. *Someone* would have noticed the President of the local chamber was using. Wouldn't they?

"Maybe," she replied simply, unwilling to start down that rabbit hole. "What else can you tell me?"

"Jesus, Holly," he said. "Are you bucking for detective? Nothing. I called what I found into Hopper and that's it."

"All right, Burt. Thanks."

"Holly?" She had the phone away from her face, getting ready to hang up, when he spoke again.

"Yeah, Burt?"

"Stay the fuck away from whatever is going on. Really. I'm off-shift in another hour and a half. I plan on going home, cracking a cold one, watching some porn, and calling in sick for the next few days."

The call disconnected.

Mr. Whiskers had made a nest on her pillow and protested when she reached over and picked him up, but quickly settled back down when she settled him on top of her stomach and began stroking him.

Rathcrog.

Carl's voice floated through her head and, as it did, she was struck with sudden worry for him. Whatever was going on appeared to have been put into motion by his conversation with Dennis Tierney. She needed to check on him. If nothing else, apologize for shutting him down earlier.

But in the morning. The alarm clock on her nightstand showed **3:43**. Her shift didn't start until seven that night, but she was drained. If she didn't get at least a few hours' sleep she was afraid she would doze off at the switchboard. Setting Mr. Whiskers back into the pillow indentation, she rolled over next to him, arm outstretched, with her hand sitting gently on the base of his tail. The end of his tail twitched as her eyes flickered slowly and the room faded.

Holly blinked.

How long…

The red numbers on her nightstand glowed. **4:26**.

She had been dreaming about…what? She tried to chase down a peripheral shadow.

A pool?

She wasn't sure. It was large and flat, but as she came fully to, the wispy outline of whatever it was disappeared back into her subconscious.

Her phone, lying next to the clock, was blinking red. Missed call or a new message. That must have been what brought her back from her exhausted sleep, as short as it had been. Climbing carefully over the purr-factory next to her, she stood and checked the cell.

Two missed calls from the Chief.

Shit.

She had never received a direct call from her before.

She hit redial and wedged the phone between her cheek and shoulder as she began pulling off the previous day's clothes.

"Thanks for calling me back, Holly. I take it you got my message?"

Damn it.

"Um...no, Chief. I saw the missed calls and—"

There was a slight chuckle under the low contralto rather than reproof. "Don't worry about it. We had a call from the Dixie. Dennis Tierney–"

"You found him! What was he doing at the supermarket?" She keyed her phone's speaker button and grabbed a uniform from her closet, hopping slightly as she pulled the slacks on.

"Holly, no, we haven't found him. Calm down."

"Right, Chief. Sorry." She sat back on the bed, one leg in her uniform pants, the other empty leg hanging limply down. Mr. Whiskers was fully awake now, head-bumping her. She pulled him over to her lap, petting him rhythmically.

"No worries. As I said, the Dixie called and said he had been a bit earlier tonight. Per the caller, he was filthy and smelling like, and here I am quoting, 'a dead racoon that shit itself'."

"Wow."

"Indeed. We have a couple of reports that his car was seen heading out of town toward—."

"Warner," she whispered, her hand stopping on the cat's back.

"Holly, it would be useful to your career if you learned not to interrupt your superiors. Not everyone is going to be as magnanimous as I am."

The cat made a disgruntled sound as she stood to attention and dumped him unceremoniously onto the floor.

"Shit, I didn't...I mean...shoot...I...I'm sorry, Chief!"

"No worries." The chuckle was above the surface this time. There was a pause Holly didn't dare break into before Hopper continued more seriously. "Yes, that seems to be the case, unless he was planning on crossing the line into Kentucky. And I've been thinking about what Carl had to say." A longer pause this time. "Well?"

"What? Oh, yes. Chief, I think Carl is right, at least in the sense that something is going on out there."

"So do I. Now, mind you, I don't buy any of that supernatural crap, but...well, Warner does seem to be tied in some way to what's happening. I'm going to head out there to take a look around, and I'd like you to go with me."

She could feel her cheeks burning. "Of course, Chief. I can meet you–"

"I'll pick you up in fifteen minutes. And Holly - how about you try to keep the 'Chiefs' to no more than a dozen a day? It's Prescott. I've told you before, we're pretty casual hereabouts."

"Yes ma'am. And I'll be ready."

There was a sigh on the other end of the phone and the call ended.

Shit.

As she finished dressing, she remembered her earlier thought to check on Carl. No way was she inviting him out to Warner, not to mention the Chief wouldn't allow it, anyway.

No, she would go over and see how he was doing when they got back. He needed the rest. God knows she could use more.

But she was a long way from being able to lie down and get some proper sleep. After buttoning her shirt, she put some dry food in Mr. Whiskers' bowl and promised him she would pick up some tuna later for his dinner. Through the window, she saw headlights pulling into the driveway.

———

She greeted her superior as she climbed into the squad car and the drive started in silence, which suited her. Silence was better than babbling like a teenager. She hated how nervous she got around the Chief, then corrected herself.

Fine. Not nervousness. It's hero-worship.

She mentally started reviewing Carl's story again, looking for anything that might help unravel the puzzle. She was deep into it, in a daze-doze, when Hopper's voice startled her.

"All good?"

"Ah...yeah. I'm good, Ch...ma'am. Thank you."

They were about two miles outside town on Richmond Road, a narrow, winding roadway indistinguishable day or night from every other road in the area. Chief Hopper put on her blinker, slowed, and pulled over to the almost non-existent shoulder, half the squad car out into the lane.

She looked at her boss in confusion.

"All right, look. This has to stop." The fortyish woman was looking back sternly.

"I'm sorry?"

"That pedestal you have me perched on."

She was sure her face would catch fire from the burning.

"I don't–"

"I said, knock it off, Holly. Look, I don't know if it's some sort of school-girl crush or–"

She forgot about the admonition to not interrupt and erupted, "I do *not* have a crush on you, ma'am."

To her surprise, the woman laughed in response. "Well, good. Although, given time to think about it, I might be a little insulted." The woman gestured a hush when she tried to interject again. "Then what is it? You do a good job. Your co-workers, even Burt Lowell, say you know your stuff. Why the deer in the headlights every time I talk to you?"

"I..."

"Spit it out, Wilmingham." An order, albeit a gentle one.

"I...I don't really know, Ch...ma'am. It's just that, well, you're a woman." She took a steadying breath and plunged ahead. "A gay woman. And I've heard about your background." At the frown from her boss, she quickly added, "Not that people go around talking about you. But it's a small town, you know?"

"Oh, I know," came the reply. "Let me guess. Local girl goes off and becomes a war hero, comes back to help her hometown?"

"More or less," she replied, not quite able to stifle the embarrassed half-smile that her ex always said gave her somewhat of a pirate look.

The frown had transformed into something more like resignation. "Figured. I won't try to talk you down from the 'hero' crap. From the outside looking in, I supposed it looks that way, although reality is a lot dirtier and more complicated." Her eyes grew hard. "But, regardless, I'm your boss. Nothing more, nothing less. The fact that I'm gay is irrelevant."

"Is it?" She heard the catch in her own voice. "Really? Morgantown is a lot bigger than Prescott but even there it's…" She couldn't finish. Too many memories of the 'jokes' as well as the outright hostility when she came out. And being bisexual had made it, she thought, even worse. As though she couldn't even make up her mind about being totally evil or not.

"Oh, I know." To her surprise, Fran Hopper smiled. "I grew up in Prescott, remember? And I've got you beat in the strikes department, being black on top of everything else. There's no way in hell I would have made the force, let alone Chief, if I didn't have the baggage of a firefight in Kandahar riding along.

I know that. As it is, I still deal with…well, we all deal with crap sometimes."

"But," the smile was gone now as a finger poked out at her, "Screw that. And screw them. You qualify, you do a good job, that's all that matters. At least," she amended, still smiling, "as long as I'm Chief. I expect you to do your job, period. And I don't walk on water, so stop acting like I do. Understand?"

She smiled to match.

"All right. I understand. And…thank you."

A nod as Hopper checked the rear-view mirror, put the car into drive, and pulled back out onto the road.

"You're welcome. Now let's go see what the hell is going on in Warner."

Chapter 6

Carl awoke with a familiar and unwelcome buzzing running through his body. It was stronger than that night of youthful drinking, but it wasn't pulling or calling him as it had back then. As he blinked the gumminess out of his eyes, he had the panicked thought that he was in a coffin, unable to see anything. As his pupils dilated, he could make out a slight glow a few feet away. He tried his arms and legs and found they were bound. His arms, at least, were in front of him and he took small comfort in that as he scratched his crotch.

He was tilted sideways, leaning against a hard surface, particles of which stuck to his cheek when he moved. He seemed to be in a small stone alcove. Gravel underneath, pocked rock overhead and to the sides.

He debated trying to stand. Besides his head, he was sore, especially the shoulder Dennis had dug into.

Dennis!

He remembered exclaiming when the dentist grabbed him, and then seeing a fist traveling quickly toward his face, but that was it, before he had come to here. Wherever here was.

But he then realized where he must be.

Warner.

That would also explain why the buzzing wasn't pushing him toward something. He was already right where it wanted him.

But what was 'it'?

Rathcrog.

He still didn't know what it meant, but the word would do for now. He wondered what it wanted, then realized it didn't matter. Escaping Tierney, and Warner, did. Get out, get hold of Frannie. warn her that whatever was going on in the town, whatever had been sleeping in Warner, was now awake.

He rocked away from the wall, stomach muscles long unused except to assist in his all-too frequent bouts of constipation, straining as he did. Upright now, he leaned forward, slowly poking his head out of the opening to the aborted side tunnel he appeared to be in.

The path to his right quickly faded into blackness. To his left, the glow grew, a large opening less than ten yards away that appeared to lead into a large room.

A shadow passed over him as he heard crunching on the gravel from the direction of the opening.

He tamped on his initial urge to call out for help. Whoever was there was playing for the other team, guaranteed.

I have to be tricky.

Unfortunately, a life of selling insurance policies had prepared him to be neither tricky nor stealthy. As he tried sliding out of his den, the small stones beneath him dug painfully into his knees and made shifting sounds that were echoed by the cave itself.

He looked at the cavern opening again and saw the shadow growing larger. A backlit figure appeared in the entryway and stepped through into the tunnel.

"Pamela? Oh, thank God. Listen, we–"

He cut himself off as the figure came into full focus. The jeans weren't as dirty as Dennis's clothes had been, but there were small tears and stains scattered across them. Above the pants, semi-flaccid breasts hung down, bare to the mine air. But it was the flesh itself that caused him to moan, "Oh God." Crusted-over fine lines and some sort of script ran from the shoulders down across the breasts and stomach. He felt gorge rise as his eyes traveled over the breasts and saw the left nipple was missing, a still moist hole where it should have been.

The shambling figure started toward him, and he lurched backwards into the anteroom in a visceral reaction to the state of Pamela Hotchkins. A sound accompanied his backward shuffling that, if he had realized he was making it, would have reminded him of the cry made by a rabbit caught in a trap.

The former Chamber president matched the sound an octave higher, and he felt the vibration in his head increase.

She began swaying slowly, still approaching, a plastic jug dangling from one scarred hand. There was a whiff of putrification, and he attempted to move further back, but ran up against the tunnel wall.

He tried to speak again, but couldn't get anything out through his constricted, dry throat. He forced a swallow and tried one more time.

"Pamela, please. I don't know what he has done to you, but I can get you help. We have to…"

His last attempt at a rational statement died as the edges of her mouth pulled up, highlighted in the back light from the outer cavern. The small, intricate etchings across her cheeks ran to the corners of her lips.

As she slurred out, 'Raa-crahh' through a hellish caricature of a smile, he saw into her mouth.

Blackened gouges ran around the gums, backed by small, serrated points, their bright whiteness contrasting with the soft glow filtering into the space, making the light appear dull.

His mouth opened and closed like a landed trout. Still grinning, the creature stepped forward and grabbed his wisps of hair, then tipped his head back. The plastic jug was raised, and she poured it down onto his face and into his gasping mouth. He tried shaking his head free and nails dug into his scalp, holding him in place. Choking, most of the water sputtered out of his mouth, dribbling down into his lap.

Most. But not all.

Chief, we have another Tierney sighting. About twenty minutes ago, his car was seen on the south side of town. Want me to send out Fred and Larry to canvass the area?

Holly didn't think they would find him. Warner was south of town.

Apparently, Chief Hopper had the same thought.

"Negative, Callie. Have them meet me out at the pull-in for Logger's Road."

"You got it."

"Hopper, out."

Turning to her. "Well?"

"He's heading to Warner," she replied more calmly than she felt.

"Agreed." They turned onto the shoulder at the intersection of Logger's.

The car stopped and Hopper pushed a button under the dash. The trunk popped open.

They stood behind the cruiser. Hopper pulled a double-ought from the embedded rack on the floor of the trunk and Holly reached down to grab another shotgun, but Fran's hand reached out and rested on top of hers, stopping her.

"No," was the reply to her questioning look. "Mind you, I'm still doubtful of Carl's fairy tale, but someone killed Bird and Dennis Tierney is the prime suspect as of now. I'll handle the crowd dispersal part of things. You qualified Expert, didn't you?"

She felt a flush that her boss remembered. She said, "Yes."

Nodding at her, Hopper said, "Better than anyone else on the force, including me. Grab the Colt," gesturing at a rifle strapped in next to the shotguns.

The weapon was a slightly more mobile version of the Army XM-7, which had replaced the long-standing M-16, and was intended for precision shooting.

She dipped her chin in acknowledgement and unclipped the rifle. She grabbed two magazines from the mounted ammo box before slamming the trunk shut.

Another cruiser pulled in and parked behind Hopper's and inside it she saw the two officers that had been out at the Baxter fire earlier.

Fred Larch, a ten-year veteran of Prescott's finest and pushing forty, and Larry Welkins, a decade older, exited the vehicle and greeted them.

"Thanks for coming," Hopper said. They were used to her overly polite ways and nodded.

"What's the plan?" Welkins asked.

"We'll take the cruisers in as far as possible, then hoof it into Warner. Tierney was spotted heading this way. At this point he's a suspect in Travis Bird's murder, but even if he isn't the perp, he may have information about it, and the fire, at Banyon Lake." Fred looked excited, Larry not so much. It was he who asked, "Isn't it possible he's back at Banyon? Scene of the crime type thing?"

Hopper hesitated. "He could be. But something tells me he's here unless he crossed state lines. Call it a hunch."

Fred said, "I'll take your hunches over a hell of a lot of things, Fran."

He received a nod in return and he and Fred got back into their cruiser, Holly and Chief Hopper into the Chief's. A bumpy mile down the pitted and washed-out trail and they stopped once again. They had bottomed out a few times on the way and the headlights showed it got worse up ahead.

The four officers exited the vehicles and lined up across the old road. Fred and Larry were off to the left, a fifty-foot gap between them, each with sidearms unholstered. Chief Hopper stood next to her cruiser, the shotgun dangling casually at her side. Holly walked off into the low growth brush to the right, carrying the Colt. Flashlights were out and on.

"Let's get to it," Hopper called out, and they started a slow march toward the former town.

There was the Source, and that was enough. Memories, pain - irrelevant. The Source provided all that was needed. He was no longer Carl Miller, retired insurance man. He was simply the *Acair*, the *Anchor*, performing needed tasks for the glory of the Source.

And he was content for the first time since the death of his wife.

He shifted his hands on the gas-powered jackhammer's handle. Between the blood and sweat, the four remaining fingers on each hand tended to slip.

A feather touch on his back caused him to turn around. The *Fuilier*, once Pamela Hotchkins, was holding something out to him. He took it without acknowledgement, and she walked back down the tunnel. His stomach had been growling for well over an hour and the pain had started a short time after that, but he had ignored it. Now, he understood it was time to eat.

There was much work still to be done, and his vessel could not be allowed to collapse from weakness.

He chewed, the meat and blood giving him a shadow of pleasure. When the flesh was gone, he reached into his mouth and pulled out two small bones. He continued his mastication for a short time, then spit into his palm.

He looked absently for a moment at the thumbnail in his hand before dropping it to the cavern floor. Turning to the jackhammer he had leaned against the cave wall, he wrapped his fingers around its handle, positioned it against the trough he had already created, and pulled the trigger.

A part of his body that had been long dormant filled and came to attention as the vibration from the hammer rumbled, but he focused on the job at hand.

Chips of rock dislodged by the hammer flew, some cutting his face, but he didn't waver.

There was work to do.

***

Holly didn't have an innate fear of the dark or the woods. She and her father had spent enough weekends, and occasionally entire weeks, camping out at Cooper's Rock State Park that she was used to dark forests.

But this was different. The closer they got, the more she felt the need to swivel her head, looking for she didn't know what. And her nipples were rock hard, pressing against her sports bra. She knew there was lotion in her future.

If there is a future.

She told herself to stop the nonsense, doing her best imitation of her mother, a woman who had grown up in a three-room tarpaper shack and was not big on either self-pity or fear. There had been a murder, yes, and a grisly one. But that didn't mean the world was ending.

But there's something...

"Over here!"

That was Fred. She swerved left and walked quickly across the roadway behind the Chief, making up for her own shorter strides by pushing hard.

She came even with Hopper a few feet short of where Fred stood looking down, poking something with his boot.

A half-buried pinecone.

"Good job, Fred." Larry kicked at the forest refuse. "You've solved the case." She stepped between the two men, muttering 'Asshole' in Larry's direction, momentarily forgetting Hopper's presence. When she realized the Chief was just behind her, she glanced back in a bit of panic. Hopper's expression was hard to make out in the reflected flashlight beam, but she thought there was a curling up of the woman's lip.

"Hard to make things out at night," Hopper said.

"Yeah," Fred said, embarrassed. He stepped back from the pinecone and looked toward Warner.

Hopper said, "Spread back out and let's keep going."

They had been walking again for about ten minutes, the going rougher the closer they got to Warner, with mounds of dirt overgrown with scrub, and piles of brush scattered along the way. Holly guessed as the town expanded over time, the forest remains had simply been pushed to the newest outskirts.

"Hey, gl--!"

Fred again. She hoped for his sake it wasn't another pinecone. Aside from the additional grief Larry would give him, and she was sure the latter would be sharing the tale around the squad room before his next shift ended, the Chief's patience was not unlimited.

Without waiting for a signal this time, she cut over toward the roadway. She was wearing down and didn't bother to attempt to catch up with the Chief this time.

Larry reached his partner first.

"Jesus! Chief! Oh, my fucking God! Fran! Hold on, Fred. Fuck! Frannie!"

Something she had never heard, nor expected to hear, from Larry. Fear.

No, not fear.

Pure terror.

At an instinctual level, she wanted to high-tail it back down the roadway to the cruiser. In fact, her body began turning that way when she saw Chief Hopper up ahead start running toward the voice.

She overrode her body and began running after the other woman. Hopper stopped next to Larry, who was hugging Fred around the waist, sobbing. The other man stood silently, swaying slightly.

When she reached them, she noticed Fred wasn't so much standing silently as floating, feet just brushing the ground. His back was to her, and there were lumps surrounded by dark spots across the back of his uniform. Larry, still holding onto his partner, slid to the ground, kneeling in front of Fred.

She stepped around closer to Hopper to see what was going on.

"Larry, stop." Chief Hopper's quiet tone was firm but compassionate.

"Damn it, Fran, help me!" Holly saw he wasn't actually hugging Fred, but trying to pull him loose from the small log that seemed to be stuck to the front of his uniform. Her eyes scanned the chain wrapped around the log that ran up into the dark forest canopy.

Confused, she was about to ask what had happened when she saw that the other end of the log had long pieces of metal, rebar spikes from the look of them, sticking out of the wood.

With a sick feeling, she realized the lumps in the back of Fred's shirt were the ends of more rebar. They had punched through his shirt and chest, leaving wet sticky spots around them, and extended through his body.

Vomit filled her mouth, and she turned away. Through the sounds of her heaving, she heard Hopper's voice become sharp.

"Larry, he's dead. There isn't anything you can do." Compassion turned to ice. "Except help me catch the bastards who did it."

Larry Welkins, who had ridden with Fred Larch since the younger cop had joined the Prescott force fresh out of the Academy, continued to cling to his partner's legs, the snot on his face highlighted by Hopper's flashlight beam.

"Larry, up now!" Holly hadn't heard the Chief use this sharp, commanding voice before but knew she would have snapped straight to attention if it was directed at her.

It did the trick. Larry rose, snuffling and pulling himself up on his dead partner's pants, which started to slide down.

Upright, he turned to Hopper. There was a dangerous light in his eyes and she saw his hand ball up as he shouted, "You fucking black bitch, you brought—"

Hopper dropped the shotgun and stepped forward, a foot going between Welkin's spread legs. One hand snaked out, grasping the fisted arm just above the wrist. She didn't quite see what happened next except the result, which was Larry on the ground, arm twisted behind him, Hopper's knee in the small of his back.

He rolled, trying to free himself, then cried out as the Chief used her free hand to poke a spot just above his trapped elbow. That ended his struggles.

All right, it's official. I do have a crush on her. Jesus, that was-

"Holly, I'd appreciate it if you would get my gun and also take Larry's sidearm for safekeeping." The tone was the same one she used when stopping at Holly's desk to ask about some paperwork.

Putting her rifle behind her, she used her foot to push the shotgun next to the Colt. Leaning over the prone man, she unsnapped Larry's holster and removed his Glock, shoving it into her waistband. Then, noticing Fred's slowly rotating body also had its sidearm holstered, she stepped over to it and removed his gun as well, sliding it next to Larry's. She backed up and picked up both the shotgun and her own rifle.

"All set, Chief," she said as Hopper stood, pulling Larry up with her, one hand on his shoulder, the other maintaining a grip on his wrist.

"Thank you, Holly." Then, to her surprise, the Chief released Larry, who stood limply, head hanging down. The man's anger had drained away, and he looked a decade older than he had a little while before.

Just in case, Holly switched the shotgun to her left arm, cradling it and the rifle together, and rested her right hand on the butt of Fred's gun; she took a step to the side to give herself a clear sight line. Hopper noticed, but stayed silent.

Hopper spoke quietly. "Now, Officer Welkins, your partner is dead and there isn't anything that's going to change that. But whoever rigged that log is out there somewhere, maybe in Warner, maybe back in Prescott. And that's something we *can* do something about." Her voice was dead of winter now. "We can catch the sick scum who did it and make sure they pay." The dark hand that had whipped out a little while before, keeping him from ending his career, reached out this time in offer.

Larry didn't move for a moment, then his head came up slightly and his own pale hand grasped hers.

"I...I'm...sorry, Chief."

The woman squeezed his hand and dipped her head in acknowledgement, but said nothing.

"Chief, come in. We have a problem."

Hopper pulled her hand back and clicked her lapel mic.

"I'm here, Callie. What's going on?"

"We had a report of something strange out at the Twisted Kitty a couple of hours ago. Multiple people called in and said it's closed, although all the lights are on inside."

Hopper looked at her, then at Larry as the latter mouthed, *On a Saturday?*

"Definitely odd, Callie, but I'm assuming you aren't calling to just report on a closed bar?"

"No, Chief. I sent Burt over. He complained about it since he was just getting ready to wrap up for the night, but with everything that's been going on, he was it until first shift comes on."

The dispatcher seemed to be trying to explain her rationale and short-circuit any complaints Burt might make, which Holly was certain he would.

"No worries, Callie. What did he find out?" *"Well, that's it, Chief. I don't know. He checked in when he got there, but never closed out with me. I tried him a few times but no response. It's been over an hour now and I was getting ready to send Sam and Hollis over, since they finished up out at the Baxter place."* Sam and Hollis were, Holly knew, the other two nightside officers. *"Considering everything that's happened tonight, though, I wanted to flag you first."*

"Much appreciated. Go ahead and dispatch them. Let me know what they report. Anything else?"

"Just some standard nuisance calls that I'm juggling between things."

"Fair enough. Also, Callie, we're going to need Marshall out here when he's done at Banyon." She looked up the roadway, back toward where the cruisers were parked. "Roughly two miles in from County 102, heading toward Warner. He'll have to hoof it, so send someone with him to help carry. And upgrade that BOLO Tierney to include 'suspect, armed and dangerous'."

"Shi–Will do, Chief." Callie said. She didn't ask for details on the death out by Warner.

"Thanks. Hopper out."

Her boss turned to her.

"Any bets that Tierney paid a visit to the Kitty?"

"No bet. But I still don't understand why he killed Bird or did this." She gestured toward Fred's body, which continued to turn slowly. She added, "Assuming he did."

Another nod. "Assuming he did, but either way, he is the prime suspect at the moment."

Larry said quietly, "Chief?" and gestured with his shoulder toward his partner's body.

Round and round we go.

Hopper nodded. "Let's get him down."

As the Chief wrapped her arms around the former patrolman's waist and she grasped the ends of the log, Larry came to life, a panicked look on his face.

"Wait."

He stepped in front of Fred and, hand trembling slightly, closed the dead man's eyes before stepping back.

With Hopper holding the corpse steady, she pulled back hard on the log. She felt a twist in her stomach as it came loose with a sucking sound and the Chief laid Fred Larch on a bed of pine needles.

Glassy-eyed, Larry turned to their boss.

"Let's find the son of a bitch."

Chapter 7

Burt was not happy. After the call from Holly, he had finished his rounds, zigzagging across Prescott, trying not to think about Hotchkins' house. He was on his way to clock out at the station when Callie called, asking him to go out to the Kitty.

Last fucking thing I need tonight, he thought.

But here he was. He unclipped his seatbelt and grabbed the mic from its hook.

"Onsite, Callie. I'll let you know after I deal with whatever bullshit needs dealing with."

He stepped out of his vehicle, unsnapping his holster. Long habit caused him to scan the parking lot, and he noted there were fewer cars than normal for a Saturday night, even if it was officially Sunday morning now. Climbing the steps to the entryway, he registered the 'Closed' sign that had caused his end of shift to go to hell in a handbasket. Through the door window, he noticed the lights were on inside and even the dance floor in the back was illuminated.

What the hell?

He pulled on the door, and to his surprise, it opened.

It looked like the set of a bar scene from a movie that hadn't started filming yet. The tables scattered around the wooden floor were rife with glasses, ranging from full to dregs and clear to amber, along with partially eaten plates of wings, bowls of nuts and popcorn, and similar pub fare. Rainbow colors from overhead strobes swirled across the worn floor leading to the kitchen entrance.

His hand, seemingly of its own volition, had moved to grip the Glock. Scanning the empty room, he stepped slowly toward the back.

There was a dark pool that started at the edge of the dance floor that was just before and off to the side of the swinging saloon-style kitchen entrance. He froze when he saw it, and his hand tightened on his gun. There was a thin, viscid rivulet that had filled a groove in the floor, a thick drop of it hanging into the separation between boards.

Just fall, for Christ's sake.

He started to reach for his personal radio to report in when he heard it - someone humming. Cheerfully and rather absently, like a person engaged in a repetitive but necessary task, keeping themselves company as they completed their work. His father, who used to build furniture on weekends to supplement his glass factory wages, would hum as he pumped an old wooden lathe.

He suddenly wished he was still nine, sitting on a stool next to his father, watching him work.

But he wasn't, and this wasn't a middle-aged man's workshop. He also doubted anyone was making a rocker in the Kitty's kitchen.

He pulled his Glock free of the holster as he walked forward, pointing it slightly toward the floor He stopped just short of the puddle.

"Who's in there?"

There was a pause, then the humming continued unconcernedly.

"Hey, I said who's in there? Come out slowly!"

There was a longer pause this time, but then the tuneless song started again.

He muttered *Fuck* and stepped around the blood.

There were more puddles, and splatter, in the kitchen. Most of it, though, was on and around a meat slicer mounted to the butcher block counter running down the middle of the room. Stringy flesh hung from the bent blade. Apparently, it hadn't been up to the job.

Stacked next to it was an assortment of body parts. The Kitty's owner, Rufus O'Brian, smiled up at him from the counter, an expression Burt had never once seen on his face, dating back to when they attended junior high together. He wondered what Rufus had to smile about considering he was missing the bottom five and a half feet of his body; his current height ending in dangling, ragged strips of skin and veins a few inches below his chin.

And there were more heads, multiple stacks making pyramid shapes against one wall, like twisted endcaps of vegetables at the Dixie. Bile burned in his throat as he scanned the faces, each with a permanent serene expression.

Shirley Hempstead, Frank Hempstead, Hock Luth, Lila McDonell, Claire Smith, her six-year-old, Aiden...

"Hi!"

He jerked, his gun swinging around to point toward the voice. In a shadowed back corner was a prep table up against a large stove, its eight burners dormant.

A man with a thin-bladed knife in one hand stood behind the table. On the table lay a human arm with fingers curled upward, the arm's visible raw flesh explained by the pile of folded skin next to it.

There was blood smeared up one cheek and all around the man's mouth. A small piece of skin hung at one corner of his lip, and Burt swallowed hard.

"Dennis Tierney, you're under arrest." He was glad the gun didn't waver. God knew he felt like his whole body was shaking.

He didn't add any specifics to his pronouncement, partly because he was afraid if he kept talking, he would vomit. Also, whether Tierney was responsible for the murder of Pamela Hotchkins or Travis Bird, the current scene was enough to put the psycho away for the rest of his life. He only wished West Virginia still had the death penalty.

"Sure thing." Tierney put down the knife and stood slowly, stretching his shoulders. "I need a break, anyway. Long night, you know?"

He gave a secretive smile, and Burt wiggled his gun.

"Don't move!"

"Hey, no problem." Tierney squinted a little at Burt's chest, taking a step forward. "Officer...Lowell, is it?"

He didn't respond but clutched the Glock tighter, his eyes unable to leave that tiny left-over piece of someone's life dangling from the dentist's face.

"I said don't move!"

"All good, Officer." Tierney raised his hands. "Listen, question for you. Did you know a deli slicer can't handle bones?" He laughed, "I know, right? I figured 'zip, zip', done deal." A chagrined shake of his head as he took another small step. "But no. Damn thing choked on the first one. Luckily, Rufus there," he gestured with one of his upraised hands, "runs a well-equipped kitchen."

Burt's eyes left Dennis's for no more than a second, glancing at the severed head next to the slicer, but it was enough for the other man to reach behind his back and pull out a cleaver. Burt squeezed the trigger of the Glock, but the top-heavy blade was already spinning through the air.

Thwack!

The bullet had gone wide, and Tierney stepped forward, looking down at the Prescott policeman whose fingers grasped at nothing, pistol lying next to him. He braced himself on Burt's sternum, looking interestedly at the blood and foam forming around the fallen man's lips. The cleaver came loose with a hard yank. The dentist licked the length of it.

Burt was gasping helplessly, hands still reaching for a salvation that would not come. Tierney smiled again and whispered, "All good."

The blade came down again.

Dennis Tierney, former dentist, now *Scribner* for the power that filled him, was content. More than that, he was fulfilled, something he was previously familiar with only second-hand.

He had always thought of himself as more a salesman than anything and had a buried sense of shame over it. His father had sold used cars back in Bridgett at Sunshine Cars before the owner converted it to a trailer park and flea market, and he remembered the comments from adults, as well as other kids.

Rip-off artist!

Thief!

Hey Dennis, what's the difference between a politician and your father? Every once in a while, a politician tells the truth!

So, he went into dentistry. He hadn't been bad at it. Not really. Granted, his practice had been mostly first time, and single visit, customers, but it was successful enough to afford regular presents for a string of mistresses and a decent house in a new housing development.

Now, though!

He had been Chosen. And when his work was done, everyone would recognize it was he that had been instrumental in bringing contentment to all the people of the world. Not that they deserved it, considering it had been a small group of them that had banished it an eon before. But the Source was magnanimous and didn't hold grudges. Unlike him.

He pictured Amanda and Carol supine at his feet after drinking of the Source, and what he would do to them.

Chop!

His left eye closed reflexively as blood spattered upward. He set the cleaver down and wiped it clear. No accidents, not even a scratch, could be allowed. Unlike the other vessels, his must remain intact. It was their role to act as conduits, his to read aloud the sacred words, returning the Source to its rightful place.

He pushed a torso off the table, its blue shirt open to the navel, the badge engraved with "Lowell" still attached. Unfortunately, the torso was unusable due to a large dragon tattoo across the chest. It *thunked* to the floor, joining other assorted parts deemed unclean because of tattoos, stretch marks, and other imperfections.

The doorway must be pure. Unblemished.

The skin from the leg came free with a ripping sound. He laid it on a tall, teetering pile off to the side and took a deep breath.

All good.

Strategy isn't your problem, it's the Captain's. Focus on tactics. What's your next step? Keep an eye on your surroundings. Does your partner have your back? Don't lose focus, it will kill you!

Holly was flashing back to a class and exercise at the Academy. They had been driven to an empty lot on the outskirts of Morgantown, where plywood facades mimicked the outside of buildings. These augmented the three-story remains of an abandoned tenement. An instructor took the part of a suspect barricaded in the building, along with an unknown number of associates and hostages.

She could see Fran Hopper off to one side and making her way down the overgrown road. About a dozen paces past the Chief in the woods, she could just make out Larry's outline.

She gave him credit. After losing it on the Chief he had pulled it together, more or less. Better than she would have in his place, she was certain. She had barely known Fred and was still pretty rattled.

So what are you doing out here?

Even in her own head, the question was rhetorical.

The Chief had asked her to come with her. She didn't know about the bowels of Hell, but she would go at least as far as the doorway with the woman and take it from there.

Doorway.

She saw an image of cloth of some sort, covering an entry way and shivered.

What is Rathcrog?

Chapter 8

Carl's heart was fluttering in his chest, but he continued working. It wasn't until the noise in his head changed cadence that he released the trigger on the jackhammer and stepped back, away from the growing cavity in the wall. He examined it for a moment, pleased with the symmetry of its shape and his careful placement of stones around its edges to ensure stability. Then, he felt a twinge of shame at the speed of his work, but was reassured by the buzzing. He had been Chosen as *Acain*, the *Anchor,* and had an important role to fulfill. His strength must be conserved.

He put the stub of one thumb into his mouth, sucking like a toddler. There was pain, but that was to be ignored. He used his teeth to peel the still wet scab that had formed and sucked on the once again free flowing blood, feeling its strength course into his vessel.

The newest Chosen approached. He had a momentary flush of pride that he was selected before her but was reminded that

"

each had their role to fulfill, each important in its own way. He murmured a silent apology, then responded to her presence.

"Yes?"

The former Twisted Kitty waitress held out her hands.

He allowed her to take the jackhammer, and she stepped awkwardly forward to take his spot.

The Stríocálaí restarted the hammering. He knew it was only another foot or so and they would be through to the trickle that started far beneath the surface and ran to Banyon Lake, local summer water-sport haven and the reservoir for Prescott.

Almost time, he thought as he gnawed at a small piece of loose hanging skin.

The *Fuilier* came into sight from the tunnel leading to the outside, the body etchings in relief to the light floating upward from the Source.

Without speaking, she joined the Stríocálaí and, jackhammer laid aside, they began pulling down the dislodge stones. He stood and, not hearing a mental admonition, picked up the jackhammer again and went back to work until the *Fuilier* made a mewing sound that he felt more than heard; he stopped his hammering. The last stone she pulled free had revealed an empty darkness behind it. The three leaned in, heads touching, and heard the gentle sound of running water behind and below the opening.

They looked at one another and smiled, then resumed digging.

***

The *Scribner's* head snapped up from his work and he looked off into the distance.

Good.

Things were on track. With the exception of a ripped garbage bag as he and the former Twisted Kitty waitress disposed of the unusable portions of Travis Bird, the night had gone well. Even the arrival at the bar of one of Prescott's finest had not been unexpected and yielded some usable vellum.

His tongue poked around his mouth. The original, relatively useless, teeth had all fallen out, their replacements angled slightly outward. Earlier in the evening he had felt something new. A stretching and shifting in the rear of his mouth where the throat began. And something growing, both top and bottom.

Now the growth seemed to have stopped. His tongue ran around new, sharp edges and he flexed muscles that hadn't existed a day earlier. As he did, he opened his mouth and *pushed*.

A second mouth stretched out from ligaments, extending from the inside of his jaw. Smaller than his primary mouth, a double row of slightly bowed, serrated teeth ran around its perimeter. As he pushed, the new organ moved to an inch or so just behind his primary teeth. He stretched the muscles further, and the mouth cleared his lips. He thought the new muscles must need a workout to reach their full potential and received a mental thrum of agreement.

Clicking both sets together, he pulled his new appendage back into his body, then stretched it into the open again, repeating the exercise as he picked up the filet knife and returned to his skinning. Another hour and he should be able to return to Warner to prepare for the ceremony.

CHAPTER 9

"What a cluster-fuck."

Holly wondered if Larry was British under the veneer of his peckerwood accent. Cluster-fuck didn't even begin to cover the night's happenings.

They were now walking within a few yards of each other, Hopper still on the roadway, she and the patrolman just off each side. There had been no conversation about it, but as the three cut the distance to the tree line surrounding Warner, the distance between them had also shrunk.

There had already been two close calls prior to Larry's exclamation, one about a half-a-mile back, when she had called out 'Stop!' after her beam of light reflected off something just ahead of her.. Another tripwire that led back a few feet to a tree where two branches acted as a trigger to release another spiked log hanging overhead. The second, a similar set-up spotted by Larry a few minutes later.

The current trap that caused him to come out with his understatement now lay before them. Chief Hopper had called out 'Halt!' When she and Larry stepped toward her, the woman had added, 'Stay behind me.'

Hopper was toeing scattered leaves in front of her, clearing them from a patchwork of branches that covered a hole in the middle of the roadway. The Chief nudged the branches closest to her and they fell into the concealed pit below them. Below, sharpened sticks stood upright in the sandy soil.

The sight of these was what caused Larry to share his opinion of the situation.

"That it is," Hopper said agreeably. She shined her light around the edges of what they could now make out as a bit too regularly shaped covering of leaves, then began walking carefully just outside their outline, putting one foot out at a time to test the ground before stepping. Making a full circumference, the Chief went back to where she and Larry stood, neither having dared to move in the meantime.

"Someone definitely doesn't want us visiting Warner," Chief Hopper mused.

"No shit." She didn't notice at first that she had sworn in her response to Hopper's comment. It wasn't until the Chief said, "Loosening up, I see, Holly."

She saw Hopper's grin and bit off an apology, smiling in return.

Instead, she said, "Keep going?"

Simultaneous from Larry, "Backup?"

Chief Hopper nodded, apparently to both, and keyed her radio. "Callie, come in."

After receiving confirmation, Hopper said, "I need you to contact the trooper barracks in Morgantown and request a tac squad. Provide them with all current information. Then pull everyone in that's in or near Prescott. I don't care if they're off-shift or on vacation. Have them rendezvous at the station with the state squad. Officer in charge will be the head trooper until they're able to join up with us, but you need to be clear on this - have them keep to the road on the way in. Someone has left some nasty surprises around in the woods, and I don't know that we found all of them. Also, there is a pit on the roadway about a quarter mile outside Warner. Make sure they know to keep an eye out, so they don't stumble into it. I'll mark it along with anything else we come across as we go. When they get to the clearing around Warner, have the OC contact me. Got all of that?"

"Ten-four, Chief. Also, Marshall closed out a bit ago at the Baxter place. They found a foot and an upper arm in the brush a few feet from where the thigh was. All showed signs of having been cut, he actually said 'hacked', from the body. He won't know if they were pre or post-mortem until he gets back to his lab, though. He and two of ours are on their way out to you now."

"Thanks, Callie. When they've secured the scene here, have them meet me at the end of Logger's, on the Warner end. Hopper, out."

Hopper turned to her two officers.

"Well, folks. Let's not dawdle," and headed slowly down the rubbled road.

Standing next to the pit, she and Larry looked at each other. After a moment, they followed Hopper.

The Stríocálaí *felt safe for the first time since her grandfather had died. While the other Chosen might think in terms of a buzz/humming, for her it was more of a mind-hug. And if there was a payment to be made for that hug, well, that was life. She had learned at an early age that there was no such thing as a free lunch.*

After dropping her current load of rubble off by the lengthening channel, she limped back to where the scarred, half-naked Fuilier *continued to dig alongside the* Acair. *She embraced her new role, new identity, even though she could not pronounce the word* Stríocálaí, *nor knew what it meant. It didn't matter, however. There was work to do, preparing for the ceremony. And following the completion of that work, she had been reassured her true purpose would be revealed.*

She felt another mind-hug, caught a whiff of stale sweat and coffee, and continued the clearing, letting her mind wander.

She had accompanied the Scribner *to the Twisted Kitty after ensuring her trailer was fully engulfed in flame. It had not been difficult to convince Kitty owner Rufus to let her swap out the tap water they put at every table for what she told him was 'spring water', from a source she had found on her property. Any hesitation he might have had disappeared when she hinted at her need for an experienced business partner that she was willing to give the majority of the profits to in return for help marketing what she called 'liquid gold'. He had made a snide comment about naming it after a furniture polish, but she had seen the avaricious gleam behind his eyes and knew all the waitresses would be instructed to use the jugs she lined up on the set-up station. An unexpected bonus had been him instructing the bartenders to set out the water for anyone sitting at the bar.*

It was early for a Saturday and the Kitty was only at about half-capacity, but she was told it was time and turned the door sign to 'Closed', switching off the outside lights as she did. By then, most of the customers were one with the Source. The few that had an aversion to drinking water at a bar were easily dealt with. Their screams garnered no reaction from the friends and family that had drunk from the pitchers as it was those friends and family that dealt the blows.

Then each of the living lined up to do their part, moving in a single file slowly to the swinging kitchen doors. Red, green, and yellow lights from the strobes shone down on them as they shuffled through.

The primary color once through the doors, however, was red alone.

The *Fuilier* dropped the jackhammer and picked up a pickaxe. Bare breasts bounced as she swung it in counterpoint to the old man's rather clumsy strikes, the *Acair's* lack of thumbs forcing him to readjust his grip after each blow.

A dozen more swings and it was done.

The Stríocálaí scooped up the last of the freed stones and dropped them to the side.

Squatting, the *Fuilier* hooted while the Stríocálaí and Acair gave satisfied smiles.

A channel ran an irregular path to the opening in the wall, getting progressively deeper as it approached the wall. The opposite end ran straight to the edge of shimmering water that contained the essence of the Source. Both ends were blocked by a sequence of stones.

After admiring the result of their work, the three vessels moved to the large boulder near one wall. Several slightly wrinkled toes sat on its surface, nails decorated with chipped red polish matching the polish on the Stríocálaí's fingertips. There was a brief celebratory toast, puckered flesh making no noise as the Chosen pressed the digits together.

The Stríocálaí thought the well-earned repast was better than any left-over wings ever had tasted at the Kitty.

In his previous life, the *Scribner* had never sewn so much as a sock-hole; he was gratified that he had done an adequate job with the offerings from the Twisted Kitty's terminal patrons. The work would never have won a ribbon at the Bridgett 4H fair, but he was assured that it was good enough.

The result of his efforts was piled neatly in the back seat, along with pieces of PVC and other items from the hardware store.

Ahead, two cars perched at slight angles on either side of the pull-in, noses pointed down Logger's Road. A police cruiser and a hearse. He turned off his lights and pulled in just behind the hearse.

He got out and removed the collapsible cart, the kind he had always considered an 'old lady' wagon, and quickly loaded the remaining contents of the back seat.

The night was still, and he heard faint voices somewhere farther in, but he would deal with those as needed. Cart in hand and bumping along behind him, he headed toward Warner.

County Coroner Marshall Lovell was born and bred Prescott, his family having been in the area for generations. Like Carl Miller, Meredith Baxter, and the majority of the other residents of the area, he had heard Warner stories growing up. And as with those residents, the stories told within his own family had their own distinct flavor.

His grandfather had regaled him with tales of how his own father, Lottie Crake, had single-handedly saved Prescott from a deluge of Biblical proportions after another miner, Pat Larkin, had blown a charge in the wrong place and opened up what had apparently been a sealed cavern containing an underground lake. Lottie had died, resealing the hole, preventing the flood from killing anyone else.

Marshall took pride in his family history. That, along with having worked his way up from a hospital orderly to County Coroner, resulted in an attitude that his ex-wife referred to as *high falutin'*. Others who dealt with him thought he *put on airs*, more appropriate for a visiting state senator or, perhaps,

Rufus O'Brian who, besides owning the Twisted Kitty, had also bagged ten-point bucks in three consecutive seasons. His friends didn't think in either term as he had none, simply acquaintances and workers with whom he interacted.

Not that he felt he was missing out. He had his job and weekend excursions over the state line to Mama Elise's Massage Emporium. That was enough.

The two uniformed men with him were bent over the corpse that Hopper's group had placed in the center of the roadway. He watched as they marked the surrounding area with road flares. They then worked to slide the cadaver into a body bag, their pale faces highlighted by the red glow of the sputtering flares.

He knew neither of them, except one was 'Bob', the other 'Clarence', that information gained through having to listen to their incessant jabbering with each other. No matter. In his experience, police were interchangeable cogs, more interested in the pedestrian aspects of death, not the finely grained nuances of life, death, and how the latter occurred. Not one of them with any imagination.

Except Chief Hopper, he mentally added, picturing her attractive ebony face.

He recalled running into her at a scene involving a twenty-two-year-old OD. When he arrived onsite, an officer informed him that the dead woman, Karen Reynolds, had been working at a local brick manufacturer following a layoff the previous year from a medical device company that had moved its assembly line to Juarez. The brick manufacturer had let Reynolds go a few days because of a business slowdown. She had grown up on a horse farm just outside Prescott but, per the sister who had found her when she arrived for a girls' night at the Twisted Kitty (a place Marshall wouldn't be caught dead in), Reynolds had left town after high school and headed west to become a Hollywood star. She had returned two years later, sans fame, but carrying a heavy drug habit.

As far as he was aware, Hopper didn't know the dead woman, but there she had stood, looking down at the body, which was covered by the standard issue canvass bag, a pock-marked face visible through the still open top.

He nodded brusquely to the patrolman that had shared the information, and had started toward the body, but the cop grabbed his arm. He began to protest, loudly, when he was rudely and violently whipped around.

"Shut up, now!"

It was said in a stage whisper inches from his face and he felt a drop of spittle land on his ear. He started to protest again, already formulating the complaint he would lodge about the rude treatment, but stopped when he saw the expression on the policeman's face.

The officer, 'Lowell' according to his name tag, gestured toward Hopper with his chin.

"She isn't done."

He looked over and could see Hopper's mouth moving as she stood over the body, but couldn't make out the words. He pulled his arm away from Lowell, raising his hand to indicate he wouldn't interrupt. A few steps closer and he was able to hear her.

"...work, broken and smothered for bread and wages, to eat dust in their throats and die empty-hearted, for a little handful of pay on a few Saturday nights."

From his vantage, he had thought she looked like a descending angel. Then she bent down and touched Reynolds forehead with two fingers before carefully zipping the bag closed.

She turned and gave him a slight nod of acknowledgement as she walked back to her cruiser.

He looked after her then asked Lowell, "What–"

"It's her own benediction." To the surprised look Marshall gave him came a shrug and the reply, "My father was a minister. Anyway," he looked after the Chief, "She shows up at a lot of these, particularly if the victim is on the young side." A shake of his head. "I've wondered if it has to do with what she saw in Afghanistan but..." another head shake, and he headed in the same direction Hopper had, calling back, "it's all yours now, Doc."

"That's *Mister!*"

But Lowell was gone.

Thinking back, it occurred to him that Hopper wasn't married, and he didn't remember ever hearing anything about a boyfriend. Perhaps she would be interested...

"All set."

Bob, or possibly Clarence, zipped up the bag.

"Back to my car," he directed. "I'll also need assistance getting it into the morgue."

"Sorry, Doc, the Chief wants Bob and me to meet her." He gestured down the dark roadway in the direction of Warner.

"That's *Mister,*" he said again, with annoyance. There had been no requirement of medical training when he was appointed. Since then, the law had changed, and he had attended the mandated classes, although still hadn't passed the EMT exam. He was certain the 'doctor' comments were snide reminders about that.

"Whoops." The deputy turned his face away, but he saw the smirk. "Anyway, we have our orders. You can walk in with us or wait here until we get back."

The man's tone made it clear he couldn't care less either way. Nor probably, for that matter, if he wandered off and got lost in the woods.

"How long will you be?"

An unconcerned shrug. "No idea. Depends on what the Chief says."

"Then I will return to the wagon and wait for you there." He was gratified to see a look of annoyance in return. That meant Clarence and Bob would have to haul the body back to the hearse on their own.

Gotcha, asshole.

He thought the other would argue but Clarence simply said, "Fine," turned to his partner, and they headed down the road heading toward the mining town.

It wasn't until they had disappeared over a rise that he realized they had the only flashlights. He thought of calling out but didn't want to give away the final point.

He carefully picked up a flare and, medical bag in his other hand, began the longest walk of his life.

The two officers paused at the hole in the roadway and stared down at the splintered and sharpened spikes. Bob crossed himself as Clarence spit between his fingers three times. They carefully made their way around the pit and continued toward Warner.

Both were twitchy by the time the trees began to thin. The Chief had passed word through dispatch to maintain radio silence as they approached the town. They crouched by the roadway.

"How the hell are we–"

"*Psst.*"

Bob threw himself backwards, scrambling through the dust and stones like a frenetic crab. Clarence had shot upright and drawn his revolver, pointing it toward the sound.

"Hey, calm down." A shadow approached and congealed. "It's Holly. The Chief asked me to keep an eye out for you." She looked past them, back up the road. "Where's Marshall?"

Bob stood quickly and brushed himself off. "Jesus, Holly. I almost pissed myself."

Clarence re-holstered his gun and said, "He opted for door number three and headed back to wait at his car."

She looked at them, but when no more information was forthcoming, she simply nodded.

"Ok. Let's just hope we don't need his services. The Chief and Larry are doing a perimeter check. They're due back in…" she cupped her cell phone to mute the glow, "about ten minutes. Until then, we're supposed to sit tight, stay on the road, and keep an eye out."

Bob gave an exaggerated salute. "Aye, aye, Captain," but he smiled as he said it.

"Ass," she replied.

"Holly, what's going on." This, from Clarence. "Fred killed by some fucked up booby trap. I heard there were more body parts found at the Baxter trailer, Pamela Hotchkins missing, Tierney too. Did the dentist go nuts?"

"You missed one," she said. "Call from out at Kitty. Burt was dispatched but last I knew, he still hadn't reported in."

"Fuck," Bob said, his back turned to them. She heard a zipping sound.

"Bob, what the hell?"

There was the sound of a stream bouncing off rocks. "Remember, no leaving the road?" His arms shook up and down. This was followed by another zipping sound, and he turned back around.

"So, is it Tierney?"

She hesitated.

"Come on, Holly," Clarence said.

"Probably," she finally said. "He's at least the most likely suspect at the moment."

Bob said, "I heard Hotchkins' house looked like a slaughterhouse."

"Who told you that?"

The two men laughed.

"Fine, I should know better. Yeah, it was apparently pretty bad." Then, after a moment, "Does Rathcrog mean anything to either of you?"

Clarence Edwards shook his head, but Bob Toomey responded, "What the hell?"

Her head pivoted, and she asked, "You know it?"

"Rauthcroogh," his pronunciation stretched the o's and the last syllable was more guttural than how she had said it. "My grandfather told stories…"

When he tapered off, face scrunched up in thought, she prompted, "Well?"

"Hell's Gate. He used to tell stories from when he was a kid in Ireland. Rauthcroogh was the entrance to the underworld." He turned to her. "Demons, monsters, and such." Pause. "Why? What does that have to do with what's going on?"

Hell's Gate. That's crazy. But it does make a screwed-up sort of sense, doesn't it?

She scanned the scrub field just past the trees leading to Warner proper. *Where the hell is the Chief?*

"Holly?" Clarence had a worried look on his face.

She was saved from having to decide between more ducking or trying to convince them she wasn't crazy when she saw a shadow approaching.

"Chief."

The men turned quickly.

Hopper appeared, Larry a few paces behind her. The Chief scanned their group.

"Where's Marshall?"

"Waiting back at the county wagon."

It looked like the Chief wanted to say something about that, but she simply commented, "All right, then. One or more people are in Warner. There's a street off the main drag that dead-ends at a mine entrance. Looks like it was dug out recently. Someone came out once, grabbed some equipment on the ground and headed back inside. Couldn't ID them, but it appeared to be a female. There was some intermittent flickering light a-ways down the tunnel. No vehicles that we saw, though, so I'm assuming she or they hoofed it in, same as us."

Hopper scanned their faces, then came back to Holly's.

"Any updates?" Before arriving at the woods-edge, Holly had radioed Callie and told her to keep radio silence until either she heard from Hopper, or there were sightings of Hotchkins, Baxter, or Tierney, or if one of them was in custody.

"Nothing, Chief."

Hopper nodded, frowning.

"Chief? Can I talk to you for a minute?"

Hopper looked at her carefully and said, "Of course." To Larry, "Can you bring them up to speed on the layout of the town?"

Not waiting for acknowledgement, the Chief motioned for her to follow her up the roadway. A dozen paces away from the other officers, she said, "What's on your mind?"

"I…"

"Spill it."

Deep breath. "Chief, you remember the word Carl mentioned? Rathcrog?"

"Yes." It was half question and slightly drawn out.

"I asked the guys if they had ever heard of it. Bob had. He pronounced it *rauthcroogh*.

"All right."

Something was wrong. The Chief was a little too calm, even for her.

"He said his grandfather used to tell stories about it. He was from Ireland. Bob says it means Hell's Gate."

No response.

"Ma'am?"

A slight sigh then quietly Hopper said, "You probably wouldn't guess it looking at me but I'm Irish, on my mother's side. Her grandfather, technically. He was killed in the Warner cave-in."

Her surprise kept her from responding immediately as the Chief continued, brown eyes looking into her green ones.

"My family is, Baptist." A small smile. "Appears to have skipped a generation with me but," the smile disappeared, "my mother told me stories, ones she heard from her father. Over time, they seemed to have gotten wrapped up with Bible stories. One mentioned 'Rathcroogan' and a demon waiting for its time to come again." She seemed to be channeling her mother as she continued, her voice taking on a sing-song tone.

"When the sinners outweigh the hallowed, it will return, slaking its thirst, preparing the way for the Beast."

"King James, according to a drunken Irishman." It just came out, but Hopper slapped her arm and laughed, causing the group of men to turn concernedly toward them. The Chief waved reassuringly at them.

"Yeah, that about covers it," Hopper said, her mouth quirked. "I've always put them in the same bucket as a floating zoo or a dead man getting up and chatting with people three days after he was nailed to a tree, but...it did get me thinking."

"You didn't tell Carl, or me, this earlier, out at the Baxter place."

She tried not to sound accusatory. She might have loosened up with Chief Hopper during the course of the night's events, but she was still the Chief.

Her attempt apparently wasn't successful, and Hopper squinted at her.

"That was my call, Officer Wilmingham." The Chief touched her arm apologetically. "Sorry, Holly. You're right. I didn't. The fact is, hearing the word triggered the memory, but I certainly didn't put any stock in it, aside from the fact that Baxter's grandfather was crazy."

The dispatcher lowered her voice even further than it was. "And now?"

"If you had asked me a few hours ago, I would have told you that you needed to take a mental health day for even suggesting it but.... " Another sigh. "The person we saw out by the mine? I think it was Pamela Hotchkins."

"Why didn't you grab her?" She was shocked and this time, there was open incrimination in her words. Hopper either didn't notice or ignored it.

"Larry wanted to, and my first inclination was to run out, grab her, and run back. But she was alone and didn't appear to be under duress. And something was just...not right."

Hopper seemed hesitant, something she wasn't used to seeing in the older woman.

"What do you mean?"

Hopper said, "She was naked from the waist up. Couldn't make much out, just glimpses when her flashlight moved around, but that much was certain. She looked filthy, dirt all over her upper body. Like she had been working in the mine. And she was humming."

"Humming?"

Hopper cocked her head at her. "Ever see Snow White?"

She nodded, confused.

"Not the same tune, but like that. Like someone who was going about getting important work done and happy about it. That's when I decided Pamela could wait until we had a better idea of what's really going on."

She tried to digest this, then said, "And Rathcrog? Or Rauthcroogh or whatever it is?"

A shake of the other woman's head. "I wish I knew. But, Holly?"

"Yes, Chief?"

She gestured at the rifle in Holly's hands. "You be ready to use that if things go sideways."

CHAPTER 10

Goddamn it!

The county coroner picked himself up again for the umpteenth time and fingered the hole in his pants, feeling a sting when he touched the wet gash on his knee.

He thought he must be more than halfway back to the turnoff from the county road, but with the flare spent, it was hard to tell in the almost complete darkness. In his younger years, he had read a fair amount of pioneer stories and either the stars had been brighter back then, or the authors of the supposed 'true tales' had lied through their teeth.

He sent out another curse to the two cops that had stranded him and started moving again.

What was that?

He stopped and stared ahead, which helped him not at all. A slow rotation, trying to see anything through the thick darkness, did nothing to ease his mind.

The curse was directed at himself this time.

You're in the woods, for Christ's sake. Bats, birds, foxes. Who knows what else?

That was a mistake. The *what else* possibilities roiled his mind. He resumed his plodding, feeling as much as seeing his way forward, trying to tamp down his growing panic.

A sound.

Singing?

He stopped short again and cocked his head.

Nothing.

He started his slow walk once more, listening.

Not singing. Humming.

He froze, but the sound stopped.

If, in fact, it had ever been there to begin with.

He began walking again, one foot carefully following the other, head down, watching for roots and vines.

He halted and blinked, not understanding the signal his eyes were sending to his brain.

Shoes?

He raised his head and as he did, additional images registered.

Torn pants.

Untucked and ripped shirt.

Finally, his gaze reached a face.

It was smiling at him, lips closed.

"Who the hell are you?"

He had meant for it to come out strong and firm, but the tremolo ruined the intent.

As he looked at the stranger, he realized this might be, probably was, the missing dentist.

The man continued to smile at him, his lips opening into a full-blown grin. The teeth. There was something...

He took a step back.

The man stepped forward; his mouth continued to open. It skipped past a grin and formed what appeared to be the beginning of a yawn. He got a clear view of the rows of small, sharp teeth, and felt a coldness wash over him.

He forced himself to speak again, his voice coming out in a rasp.

"Tierney, Chief Hopper wants to speak with you. She's just a little ways behind me. I strongly suggest you—"

Marshall might not have passed the EMT test, but he knew roughly how far a human mouth should be able to open. When Tierney's reached the limit of all probability and then kept going, lip edges cracking and dripping blood, he whispered, "That's not possible."

The dentist took another step toward him, his face now within inches of his own. He tried to step back again, but iron hands gripped his arms, holding him in place.

A croak. "What do you–"

The smell hit him then, one he was familiar with but only within the confines of the morgue, and then only on the rare occasions an errant fisherman or hunter was brought in after spending a week or more decomposing in the ever-damp forests of the area.

He gagged and blinked his suddenly watery eyes.

And kept blinking, trying to clear the impossible from his view.

The mouth continued to open farther than any creature's, outside the cobra family perhaps, had a right to open. That wasn't what caused his bowels to spasm and evacuate, though.

It was what emerged from the cavernous opening.

The second mouth seemed to be a separate, independent entity, moving to its own rhythm. Viscous ropes of saliva coated and hung from the double row of razor-sharp incisors that ran around its blackened gum line, the teeth clicking together. Its movement stopped a scant inch from his nose, and he felt a breath, like moist oven blow-back.

He had the insane thought it was smelling him, like a dog.

His capacity for speech left him along with his fevered mental grasping for possibilities of escape.

The mouth pulled back a few inches, and he had just enough time to understand there was no possibility of anything, anymore.

The air whistled as the mouth whipped forward.

His hunger was slaked. Not that he had paid attention to the cramps, but he had been reminded his vessel must be strong for what was to come. The food he had met on his walk in to Warner had been almost totally lacking in muscle and that, combined with the stench of its fear, had made the meal all the more satisfying.

He reached up absently and dug a strand of tendon from between two teeth as he turned on to West Street. The entrance to shaft three up was just ahead, a hazy glow leaking out from the cavern within.

Growing stronger.

He could feel it as well. The thrumming had grown in volume so much it would have drowned out all other sounds if it wasn't also somehow channeling the outside world to him.

The *Fuilier* waited just inside the entrance. As he set the cart down, she gave a slight dip of her head, then made the keening noise he had become accustomed to, the message behind it also transmitted directly to his buzzing mind.

"How many?" Another sound, this one more guttural.

"It doesn't matter." He stroked her shoulder gently. "Assemble the Rathcrooghan and inform the *Acair* to take his position." At her hoot of assent as she grasped the cart handle he added, "Carefully! There must be no gaps or tears in the vellum."

Another head dip and the *Fuilier* made its way down the tunnel, cart scuffing behind.

He went over the preparations in place in his mind, sharing them, and posed a silent question.

They were sufficient.

He had assumed the Prescott Chief of Police would make her way here at some point. The *Acair* had told him about his conversation with the Stríocálaí before she had been Chosen and that he had shared the details of that talk with Hopper. Although not concerned, it had been advisable to make special arrangements for the policewoman, based on her background.

He entered the shaft.

"Wait, Holly."

Larry whispered as he put his arm out, blocking her. Hemp sacks, some empty, some with the remains of long disintegrated food stuffs, lay strewn around the thickly dust-covered floor. They had been squatting at the edge of one of the two windows that looked down upon West Street, watching a lone figure standing just inside the cave opening. The faint glow down the cavern tunnel had increased to the point they could make out the individual crags in the dugout walls a few feet inside. The Chief had positioned herself just out of sight around the corner of an old church across the street. Holly was going to go downstairs to signal her boss and get the ok to grab the woman.

Pamela Hotchkins was as Hopper had described her, but she didn't think it was mud covering her naked upper body. It looked more like dried blood to her.

She glared at Larry for blocking her way.

He pointed up near the corner of Main Street.

A man was walking slowly, almost sauntering, down the side street toward the shaft, pulling a small grocery cart behind him. The cart was almost overflowing, but with what, she couldn't tell.

She mouthed "Tierney?" to Larry, and he nodded.

The wanted dentist's nighttime stroll continued until he reached the cave entrance. There, Pamela Hotchkins stepped forward, and the two had a brief conversation. She felt a surge of disgust as Tierney cupped the woman's naked breast and then appeared to dig at it, putting his finger in his mouth after. Hotchkins then took the cart and began pulling it into the mine.

Tierney turned toward them, and she and Larry ducked back behind the window frame, peering around its edges.

After scanning his surroundings, Tierney followed the Chamber president in.

She looked back at Larry and, at his nod, they both duck-walked to the stairs and made their way down to the street doorway where Bob and Clarence had positions.

Hopper's silhouette appeared next to the church, and the woman trotted silently across to them.

"You saw him, Fran? And I think I made out the female. Looked like Pamela Hotchkins."

"Yep." It was a reply to both Larry's query and statement.

"So, what's the plan?" Clarence asked. He looked, as her grandfather used to say, as nervous as a cat in a room full of rocking chairs, but spoke calmly. This contrasted with Bob, standing silently next to him, who seemed to be relishing the change in routine from domestic dispute and nuisance calls that normally filled his nights.

"We take him in along with Hotchkins. I'm not sure how she fits into things, but she is definitely working with him at this point."

"Chief, I don't think that's mud on her."

Eyes back to her, followed by a slow nod.

"Doesn't change anything. Never heard of Stockholm Syndrome setting in so fast, but we are treating her as a suspect. Whatever help she needs, she can get at Ridge Hill," she said, referring to the regional hospital.

"Got it."

Brown eyes studied her. "Holly, the church is a bit less than fifty yards from the entrance. Can you get a clean shot from there?"

She eyed the span between the church and mine and nodded.

"Good. Bob, Clarence, take positions at the tree line on both sides of the street with a line of sight to the shaft entrance. Make sure Tierney or anyone with him doesn't get out. Larry, it looks like the brush over to the left of the entrance should be enough to use for cover and still give you a clear view of the mine. That's yours. Once everyone is in position, stay put and wait for my signal." She looked around, making sure the group was clear on her instructions.

"Where are you going to be, Chief?" she asked. Her boss's thinking appeared to match her own. The troopers were en route but, best case, they were at least an hour and a half away. Based on that, setting up a perimeter and guarding the mine entrance was the wise choice.

Fran Hopper's response to her question burst that bubble of belief.

"I'm going to flush them out. There isn't time to wait for reinforcements. The tunnel could have shifted or partially collapsed over time and there may be other ways in our out that we don't know about. I don't want Tierney getting away and killing more people. There may also be hostages. Some of those folks from the Kitty could be in there. And I will be damned if I will sit here and let anyone else die if I can help it."

As she looked at the Chief, she saw a flatness, and something else, in the other woman's eyes. It was then that she realized it was Army Lieutenant Hopper speaking to her, not small-town Police Chief Hopper. Someone who seen things Holly hoped she herself would never see.

So while she still had misgivings, she nodded.

Right to the Gates.

At Hopper's signal, she checked that the street and mine entrance were still clear and made her way to the church, rifle in hand.

Back against the building wall, she popped the clip out to check that the magazine was full, knowing it would be, but it was something to keep her occupied, albeit only for a few seconds. They were moving into unknown territory, big time, and any sense of the familiar helped keep her nerves still.

The glow from inside the mine seemed even brighter than a little while before, but it cast shadows around the entrance; she couldn't make Larry out, assuming he had taken up his position.

She brought the rifle to her shoulder and adjusted her arm to rest it comfortably against the crook of her armpit. Centering the crosshairs on the glow, she gave a satisfied mental grunt. Hopper stepped out from the shadow of the market building and walked into the middle of the street before stopping a dozen paces from the opening.

"Dennis Tierney!"

The glow continued uninterrupted.

The Chief walked a few feet closer, hand setting on top of her holster.

"Tierney! Come out and talk!"

She kept the rifle trained on the entrance, viewing the yellow glow through the redness of the scope.

Still no movement.

"Hello?"

The voice echoed slightly as it exited the shaft, but she was certain it was female. And scared.

Hopper drew her sidearm, hanging it down against her leg and called out, "Who is that?""Meredith! Meredith Baxter! Oh God, please! Help me!"

Fran Hopper didn't move.

"Meredith? Where is Dennis Tierney?"

"I don't know, he went down into the mine. Please, help!" The voice was weaker this time.

"Come out and we can get you to safety!"

"I can't! He tied me up. I can see the edge of the entrance, though. I'm not too far inside!" Begging, now. "Please!"

The revolver came up, pointing toward the mine. Hopper's head turned slightly toward her, motioning her forward.

Rifle still sighted on the cave glow, she walked slowly toward Chief Hopper.

When she reached her, Hopper proceeded forward slowly. She followed a few feet to the right, her breath slow and steady.

"Where's Pamala Hotchkins?" Holly was glad it wasn't she that had to do the talking. She was sure her voice would quaver. The Chief's sounded almost casual.

"She's with him. Please, get me out of here. They've gone crazy." More plaintive. "They could be back any minute!"

Hopper continued calling out to the trapped woman and approached the mine. Holly followed just behind and to one side.

"How did you get here?"

"I'm not sure. I was at my house. An old guy came by and then, a little while after he left, Tierney showed up, asking questions about Warner. I remember him hitting me. I woke up here."

Hopper was now on one side of the entrance. She took a position on the opposite side.

"The old guy. Carl Miller?"

"Yeah, that was him. Please, hurry!"

"Is he here?"

"He left my place and drove off. I don't know where he is."

Hopper's gun hand waved almost imperceptibly in the direction of the bushes. In response, she saw the barrel of Larry's Glock extend a few inches through the branches.

"I'm coming in. If you're able, keep your arms up over your head."

"I can't. They're tied to my ankles."

"Then don't move. What side are you on?"

"The left. I'm in a little dug out area." They heard stones shuffling.

"I said don't move!"

Hopper had her gun in a two-handed grip now.

The sounds stopped.

"Sorry. The rocks are cutting into my legs."

The glow that leaked out into the night had a slightly dull hue, evaporating into the mountain air, but as they stepped inside the mine, the walls danced with it. Just ahead on the left, she could see another smaller opening, bathed in shadow.

"Meredith, I want you face down on the ground."

"What? I can't–"

"Face down, now!" Although low in volume, the words were a command, brooking no disagreement.

"I...ok." More shuffling from within the side tunnel. "Ok, I'm down. Christ, just get me out of here. I'm bleeding."

Hopper waved for her to stay put and stepped forward then, after a moment, took another step to face the side tunnel. Her sidearm returned to its holster.

Looking down she said, "All right, Meredith, here's what's going to–"

The ground behind the Chief heaved. A dusty, wrinkled arm emerged, and a hand grabbed Fran Hopper by the ankle, throwing her off-balance. Hopper lurched forward, hand reaching out to brace herself against the cave wall. She managed it, but the hand around her ankle held fast and for all her kicking, it didn't loosen its grip.

The stones continued to shift. Holly watched in fascinated horror as the battered and blood-spattered form of Carl Miller rose from the shallow pit, his other hand grabbing the Chief's just above the first.

Not the convivial Carl Miller she had shared drinks with hours before, nor the worried and nervous Carl Miller that had ridden with her to tell his far-fetched tale to Chief Hopper. The face was his, yes, but the smiling snarl wasn't an expression she would have ever imagined Carl having. His breathing, too, was not the quiet wheezing she had heard earlier; more a raspy, excited, almost fervid, panting.

Then she got a good look at the hands holding her Chief in place. His fingers dug cruelly into the leg, which must be how he managed to keep hold of the policewoman, both his thumbs minor, crusted stubs.

"Carl! Stop!"

He didn't seem to even be aware she was there. The rifle swung down to her side, and she leaped forward, grabbed his shoulder, trying to pull him away with her free hand.

It was like trying to move the cave itself.

"Get his hands, Holly!"

Right.

She tossed the rifle and knelt, prying at his maimed hands.

"Carl, please! You have to stop this! We're here to help. Tierney has done something to you!" Even without the opposition force of thumbs, his hands had a death grip on Hopper's leg.

There was still no reaction from him, and she thought she would have to snap one or more of the fingers to get Hopper loose when she heard movement behind her.

"Holly? Fran? Jesus, what–"

Before the last twenty-four hours the worst, and most bizarre, scenario Larry Welkins had dealt with in almost thirty years on the Prescott force had been walking in on a meth head dressed in a squirrel costume, pummeling his soon-to-be-ex girlfriend to a pulp. But he hadn't hesitated then and didn't this time. When he saw Holly wrestling with the retiree,

Hopper kicking to get free, his words cut off mid-sentence and he ran forward, diving over Holly straight into Carl.

Whatever additional strength or force filled Carl, it wasn't enough to cancel out Newton; Larry's momentum knocked the old man over and apparently unconscious, and the officer rolled past him.

The officer pulled himself to his feet and did a little bow toward her, smiling at her in somewhat amazement at his own feat. She couldn't help but grin back and looked around for her rifle, spotting it lying next to Carl's supine body.

"Very timely, Larry. Thank you." Hopper's contralto was steady as ever. She stood back and straightened her shirt.

"You bet, Chief," he said. He was panting slightly and still smiling when his teeth shattered, six inches of a metal spike appearing through the broken grin. He made a brief gagging sound, hands shimmying at his sides, then his eyes deadened and he slouched forward, but did not fall.

Shock froze her. Hopper, however, drew her sidearm in a swift, fluid motion. It had just cleared the leather holster when something slammed down into the woman's wrist and Holly heard a crack as bone broke. As the gun hit the ground, Carl suddenly popped up a few feet to her side, her rifle dangling from his hands. He staggered toward Larry's impossibly still upright form.

"Shit," Hopper grunted, pulling her arm against her body. But even as she said it, she was swinging around toward the side opening.

There was a whistle of air and a second blow landed. It was another a metal bar, ridges running up its length, hitting across her chest.

The Chief dropped to her knees and a hard-ridden woman stepped out from her ruse spot. There was a deep tear in one cheek. Simultaneous with her appearance, Larry's body fell to the stones, and Dennis Tierney stood calmly behind him, studying the scene.

Adrenaline finally burst through the shackles of her shock, and she started for the Chief.

"Holly, get out!"

No fucking way.

"That's an–"

The metal bar descended again onto Hopper's head, and she dropped to the floor.

"Fran!"

The woman, she realized it must be Meredith Baxter, stepped over Hopper's body as Carl started back toward her, the Colt rifle clutched clumsily in his hands.

Fuck me.

She turned and ran.

Chapter 11

The former Dennis Tierney examined the *Fuilier's* work. PVC pipes fitted one into another, forming an eight-foot-tall rectangle, its base buried in the gravel and extending two feet to either side across the dry ditch. In a perfect world, the frame itself would be made of bone, but he had not had the time to deflesh the offerings. He had been told it would do, however.

Varying hues of human skin, stitched together with black thread to create a single rough piece, covered its center. Holes ran around its edge with ligaments, some still wet, pulling it taut to the frame.

He knew much the other Chosen did not. The thrumming all of them felt, that gave direction and at times, induced emotions, and evoked weakness, in his case extended to actual communication, albeit this was limited to still and moving images, like a psychic newsreel.

Tierney now knew, for example, that what they all referred to with reverence as the Source was actually a prison. The *Fomórach* had come to this land, and Warner, from a place then known as the Island of the Woods, after the painted and loin-clothed Celtic settlers there had risen up and their warrior-priests had cast it out.

The *Fomórach* had initially scoffed at those efforts. It had stridden the hills from the time of the great ice, feeding as was its wont from the tiny natives that dwelled there, always being careful to leave enough to ensure a steady supply. The natives' numbers had never rivaled those of their cousins in other parts of the world, but their meat and emotions were unrivaled. When the newcomers from the eastern mountains arrived, it had looked forward to larger and more frequent culling and feasts.

But the *Fomórach* underestimated the strength and power of the settlers, although at the time it was inconceivable anything could interfere with its age-old customs. Initially the natives, referred to by the settlers as the *Leithbrá,* had warred with the newcomers, which suited it just fine, but as the *Leithbrá* numbers dwindled, the two groups of humans made an alliance to fight their common enemy. One group alone could never had succeeded, but with the lore of the *Leithbrá* supplementing the physical strength of the eastern warriors...

In the first stages of the battles that followed, the *Fomórach* annihilated the entire population of the original small statured inhabitants, and inflicted tremendous loss on the painted settlers, using its power to turn many against their own. As it fed off flesh and pain, its strength increased.

But though their numbers dwindled, the ferocity of the new warriors, who referred to the *Fomórach* as the 'devil-mouth', intensified, as did their willingness to cut down their own when one turned against his own people under the influence of the *Fomórach*.

In the final battle, near the sea-side earthen fort the settlers had constructed, the fighters surrounded it. Teeth and claws dripping vitriol tore into flesh as it tried to break through the line of warrior-priests, but it was unsuccessful. The few it did turn to its side were killed by their fellow warriors and replaced by others waiting in a secondary skirmish line.

In a ritual taught them by their now extinct allies, the battered and exhausted humans spilled their own lifeblood and spoke words whose meaning, and limitations, they did not fully understand.

But they were successful in trapping it. And as the chant continued, molecule by molecule, the *Fomórach*'s physical form dissolved. As it faded and, finally, disappeared, the Celts swore a blood oath that the *Leithbrá* would be remembered for eternity for providing them with the means to kill the monster.

But it had not died.

The words and power used had been enough to banish it from the green island, but not to destroy it. To where it was banished was not even a consideration by the warrior-priests, as long as it was *away*. Far enough to not harass them, or their progeny, again.

It had finally awakened, formless and weak, in the cavern beneath what would become Warner many centuries later, the water in the underground lake subsuming and diluting its essence and force. Through long years, it railed against the constraints, attempting to escape without success.

Then came the Forrester Mining Company.

It had sensed the workers' approach as hammers and dynamite cut and blasted through foot after foot of the rock enclosing the prison. When they broke through to the cave, it had thrown all its diminished power toward them. Of the six miners, five had shaken their heads, trying to clear a sudden ringing in their ears.

The sixth miner had looked up, smiled, and gone to the still water, dunking his head and gulping. When he was done, the water had taken on an almost imperceptible glimmer.

He turned and as one of the others spoke to him, he swung his pick, burying it to the hilt under the man's rib cage. Bracing his foot on the still standing man's crotch, he jerked the pick free as the other miners looked on in horror. One, whose young daughter would grow up to have her own family, including a girl who would, in the course of time, give birth to Francine Elsbeth Hopper, leaped forward and grabbed the handle of the mining implement but his hands slipped. A few moments later he, too, was on the ground, a seeping hole in his back.

This brought the others to life, and they scrambled up the piled stones leading to the new opening, desperately trying to get out of the chamber, no thought of cooperation as they shoved each other. Only one, Pat Larkin, made it through into the tunnel before the possessed miner reached them. Larkin ran past the men, women, and children working in the tunnel and out of the shaft. He kept running down West Street, onto Main, and didn't stop until he collapsed from exhaustion six miles later at the junction of Logger's Road and the newly named County Road, which led to Prescott. The Smith's, a farming family from Banyon Lake, found him hours later as they made their way toward Prescott on their weekly supply run.

Back in the cavern, the pick fell, again and again.

When the possessed twenty-six-year-old Lottie Crake was done, he crawled over the bodies into the main tunnel and continued his work. By the time he exited the shaft into the cooling evening air, nineteen lay dead, including four children and two women who worked as hurriers and haulers, responsible for removing tunnel debris. With each death, the faint glow increased.

And its power as well.

Not much, however; it had been without sustenance for too long. But it had enough strength now to extend its reach slightly out from the mine. Of the first few people his vessel met outside the shaft, it was able to convince two to enter the shaft and drink. Once its essence had joined with theirs, they were dispatched to assist the first. The rest added their blood to its sustenance.

Contrary to the stories handed down in the Baxter and Lovell clans, the six pm to six am shift was half over when Crake and the others heard the *phhft* of stale air as the final stone broke free from the wall separating the underground lake from the tunnel. When the day started, Warner had a semi-official population of fifty-four, including miners and families, and those who indirectly supported the mining operation and its workers. Mine management didn't live in town, of course, residing in company houses around Warner, a few in the new town of Prescott. The town residents ranged in age from two-week old Abigail Cromerty, whose mother, Cora, danced at the Warner Social Club and Recreation Hall (if asked, Cora would have said with some pride that the father was one of five regulars, more than that would have been pure guesswork, considering her popularity), to sixty-eight-year-old Will "Lucky" Holcomb who had lost a leg in the waning days of shaft two, his lifetime savings in a tin can nailed into his corner of the closet. The few coins it contained would have bought him a couple of drinks and a dance at the SoRec, if he had been able to fish them out or, for that matter, dance.

When Crake exited shaft three, most day workers and their families were long asleep, five or more filling each cramped, slatted room behind and above storefronts, and in the company boarding house. It was the boarding house he visited first. A few stirred as their doors creaked open, but most slept on, not noticing when dreams changed to never ending darkness. A handful were awake, including Cora Cromerty, who hated missing a night's pay, but the damn baby was colicky, and she could even less afford to be thrown out because of a squalling infant. From the edge of her cot, finger in Abigail's mouth trying to either soothe or muffle the cries that caused the other two women in the room to toss fitfully, she saw the spectre enter, pickaxe in one hand, chisel in the other. Before she could whisper to the drunk miner that he had the wrong room, the figure lunged toward her. The pick froze the planned chastisement, piercing her through the top of the head. The mewling baby in her lap did not notice when blood splattered onto her frayed sleeping gown and face, the dead woman's finger still in her mouth.

A moment later, the mewling ceased as well. The other occupants slid into a permanent sleep shortly thereafter.

Of the morning workers that weren't home, the rest were at the SoRec, using what passed as liquor and beer to cut through the layers of dust in their throats and lungs.

Upon completion of his work, Crake proceeded to the Hall. The acrid smell of gunpowder still lingered inside the rooming house when he walked out into the street, but the smoke had mostly cleared, as had the screams, the latter replaced with moans and gurgling attempts to draw final breaths, in defiance of holes in chests and necks.

The two Chosen who had gone to town before him had stopped on their way to the Hall at the Baldwin Detective Agency office. Baldwin supplied peacekeepers for the company and, incidentally, the town. The one man on duty there had known them by sight and greeted them with an offer to play penny ante stud.

He didn't complain when the Chosen emptied the gun cabinet of three rifles and five revolvers along with a hundred rounds for each, being too busy bleeding out on the floor with a pocketknife lodged in his neck to lodge a protest.

Mining tools were fine, but the likelihood of off duty miners being unarmed had similar odds to a SoRec dancer taking IOUs.

Crake scanned the large open room of the club and saw one of the two Chosen bringing a foot down on a woman's head. The other Chosen sprawled across a table, a growing blood stain on his back from the bartender, who had managed to get a shot off before being cut down.

The humming in his head changed tone, and Crake understood that the loss didn't matter. Once they ensured there were no survivors, the real work could begin.

As the horizon changed from black to purple with a slight tinge of pink, the population of Warner stood at four, including Crake and the remaining other Chosen.

One of the survivors was Daniel Twomey, a recent immigrant from Galway. His widowed mother had lived with him until a visit a few hours before from Crake. Although neither Daniel nor his mother was aware of it, she was a direct, if distant, descendant of Aed mac Bricc who had squeezed blood from a self-inflicted gash in his arm, helping to complete a ritual long ago on wind-swept cliffs near what would one day become Galway.

Daniel worked the night shift but had pulled an extra twelve hours that day, filling in for an injured, and now fired, worker, so wasn't due back to the mine until the following evening. When he emerged from shaft three, he had immediately gone to the SoRec, his thirst being greater than his exhaustion, but after five Forrester Ales, he had felt an overwhelming need for bed. Stopping out back of the hall to relieve himself before returning to his shared room, he had passed out under a cypress.

When he woke hours later, he had no inkling of the carnage that was wrought during his nap. He also didn't notice how quiet Warner was as he walked back to the boarding house, blearily climbing the stairs to the second floor. The door to his room was slightly open, but that wasn't unusual. Not being able to fully open it, though, was.

He pushed hard, forcing it back, wondering if his mother had dropped something behind it.

She had. Her own body.

He knew who it was, although someone not as intimately familiar with her might not have, half her face missing.

Twomey ran out of the room and banged on the door next to his. It swung open at his first blow, and he saw Mrs. O'Neil and her two children lying on a blood-soaked cot. He made a quick check of the other rooms on the floor. Ned Gunther had wounds on his hands, several fingers severed. He, at least, had awoken and tried to ward off whatever attack had taken his life.

Downstairs, he found more blood-stained rooms and bodies.

He thought to go to the Baldwin building, despised as the detectives were by most miners for their primary work as company enforcers. As he descended the stairs, though, the stillness of the street and SoRec from a short time ago finally registered.

He slipped out the back door, armed with a knife from the kitchen, and crept toward the Baldwin office. He stuck close to the walls of the other buildings on the way, warily watching for any movement.

When he reached the office and found the dead detective in a pool of his own blood, he knew whatever had happened was town wide. The gun cabinet was empty but there was a Smith and Wesson along with a sleeve of bullets in one of the desks. He tucked both into his pants.

As he made his way carefully across the street, he saw the lights were still on inside the SoRec.

One look in the dance hall window and he choked back vomit. A nearby tree took the brunt of his emptying of his stomach.

Inside the Hall, piled bodies filled the space next to the long length of the pine bar where Lottie Crake and Eli Small, both of whom he had shared many a drink with, were skinning Bonnie Rhode's corpse. They were working their way up from her ankles, the dancer's petticoats pulled up to her neck.

He leaned against the tree, trying to think. He did not know what spurred the murders, but he didn't really care. The morning shift was still more than an hour off. He might be able to warn the dayside foreman, who usually arrived a few minutes early, and together they might manage to put together a posse, but by then, the men could have left Warner.

And they had killed his mother, along with everyone else. He assumed they wouldn't have gotten as far as they had if anyone from the overnight shift had survived.

His first inclination was to kick open the swinging doors of the Hall and open fire, but he realized he was as likely to be killed as they were, not being particularly adept with guns. His family were miners these days, and historically farmers and clergy.

He decided his best bet was to lure them into a situation they weren't likely to get through. His survival wasn't even a consideration.

He left the Hall to check the rest of Warner on the off chance someone else was still alive, and came across the bodies strewn near number three. As he approached the shaft entrance, a high-pitched whine grated through his head, and he backed away. He changed course and continued past the mine to the end of West Street, stopping at the storage shed set up a dozen yards into the scrub. From it, he grabbed a dozen sticks of dynamite and stuck them into his waistband, then threw a long loop of detonator cord over one shoulder. He went back to the mine opening, repeating the Lord's Prayer on the way. After cutting a length from the cord to tie half the sticks together, he stuck one end of the remaining spool into one charge and scrambled up over the mine opening. As he finished digging a small pit to secure the dynamite bundle, he barely noticed the pain from his bloody fingers.

Back on the ground, he tossed the rest of the attached loop as far as he was able into the shaft. On the way back to the Hall, he had to stop against a building on the corner of West to let the pain in his head clear.

When he looked around the corner onto Main, he realized it had been fortunate that he had taken a break. The two other miners were just coming down the street, Crake pushing a wheelbarrow and humming merrily.

The limited light obscured the contents of the barrow, but Twomey assumed it was the result of the knife work in the saloon and felt his stomach churn again.

He pulled the Smith and Wesson from the back of his waistband and stepped into view.

"Crake, Small! Guess you missed me in all the ruckus earlier. I'm heading out to let the Prescott Sherriff know what you've done! You'll be swinging from a tree by noon!"

He ducked back around onto West without waiting for a reaction. A moment later, he heard the footsteps speed up and the crunch of the wheelbarrow keeping pace.

As he trotted toward the mine, a *twang* nearby told him they had made the turn from Main. He increased his speed; he may not have cared about surviving to see sunrise, but he damn sure wasn't going alone.

At number three's entrance, he continued to push against the increased throbbing pain and scooped up the coiled detonator cord. He unspooled it as he descended the shaft, running it against the cave wall along the way.

He had expected either pitch darkness or spots of light from any wall lanterns still burning, but a bright glow from further down the tunnel lit the way. The noise in his head was now beating away loudly, but he kept going, forcing himself to ignore the scattered corpses along his path.

To his surprise, the tunnel didn't dead end, and he realized he would need to revise his initial plan. He shielded his eyes as he poked his head through the opening, taking a minute to adjust to the light emanating from the body of water in the cavern. There were familiar faces among the bodies lying at the bottom of the rock pile and one near the water, but he had no time for mourning. There was a rock outcropping down on the left and a boulder closer off to the right. He estimated the boulder's distance, comparing it to the dwindling spool he carried. He decided there should be enough and climbed through the hole, making his way to the large stone.

Another three minutes and he was done with his trips between the rock and cavern opening, which was fortunate, as he could hear a humming from up the main tunnel. He moved back toward the boulder and waited.

He had checked and re-checked the gun, making sure it was fully loaded and cocked. When Crake came through the opening and down the debris pile, he let off a shot.

The bullet passed a foot over Crake's head and ricocheted into the tunnel.

Crake smiled and headed toward him as the throbbing in his head crescendoed, rendering him almost blind. When he thought he would drop to his knees from the pain, he heard his mother's voice, alternating Irish and English lines from a lullaby.

Ar mhullach an tí tá síodha geala Faol chaoin re an Earra ag imirt is spoirtSeo iad aniar iad le glaoch ar mo leanbh Le mian é tharraingt isteach san lios mór.

On top of the house there are white fairiesPlaying and frolicking under the gentle moonlightHere they come calling my babyTo draw him into their great fairy mound.

The hammering withdrew somewhat, enough for him to see clearly once again, which saved him as Crake brought a chisel down in a wicked arc at his face.

He managed to turn partly away, but the blow left a cut from temple to mouth, and he would sport a deep scar if he lived. Blood poured down his face as he brought the gun up and shoved it into the other's side.

Crake heaved upward as the bullet shattered a rib on its way toward his heart. Still, he managed a few staggering steps before falling into the water.

The pounding in Twomey's head became a scream, and this time he dropped to the cave floor.

He neither heard nor saw the tumbling stones as Eli Small crawled down into the cavern, the left half of his face showing bone through raw and bloody hanging flesh, the apparent result of the ricocheted bullet that missed Crake.

With a skeletal grin, Small came toward him, gun in hand. He stopped in front of the kneeling immigrant and pointed the gun at the top of Twomey's head, hammer cocked.

He never got the chance to fire.

From behind the rock outcrop Francis Gill emerged, pulling himself up on the stones, his breath whistling through the hole in his lung, then out through the pickaxe wound in his back. From a prone state, he had seen Small come through into the cavern and managed to stand and lumber forward as the possessed man approached Twomey. Gill had no weapon and little life left but as Eli Small smiled down at Daniel Twomey, fixated on his quarry, he fell toward Twomey and grabbed at one of Small's legs, causing Small to lose his balance.

Daniel Twomey's head shot up and through pain-laced eyes saw the teetering. He lunged forward and brought Small down on top of Gill.

There were no words, no strength for them. They were in a deadly pig-pile, Twomey on top, Gill on the bottom, arms wrapped around Small, trying to keep him from getting up or using the gun he still had in his hand. Daniel heard the whistling of Gill's faltering breathing but didn't recognize it for the death rattle it was. He reached back, hand feeling around for his dropped revolver. His hand closed on its grip, and he rolled off Small. On his knees, he cocked the gun and tried to aim around the gasping Gill.

He fired, pulling the hammer back again and again, squeezing the trigger after each, until there was a hollow click, and the weapon was spent.

The other half of Eli Small's face disappeared in a cloud of smoke and red spray.

Panting and almost blind with stabbing physical and mental pain, Daniel crawled to Small and pulled him off Francis Gill, who simply lay there staring up, shallow breaths becoming more infrequent. A moment later, and they ceased.

Daniel caught his breath, and he heard his mother's voice again. It was reassuring, and dulled the roar to something not quite as debilitating.

He was amazed he was still alive and made a vow to say a prayer at St. Mary's twice a week for a year for Francis Gill. As he slowly got to his feet, he heard the lapping of water behind him.

He turned and saw the prone body of Lottie Crake twitching on the shore, head still submerged in the bright water.

There was a gulping sound, and Twomey hoped someone would have prayers said for both Gill and him.

The ends of the two cord lengths, twisted together, were still where he had placed them, tucked back against the wall by the boulder. He fumbled in his pocket and came out with a match.

The sound of stones moving behind him was louder now, as was the white noise in his head. His mother's voice faded. The match sizzled when he struck it down the rock wall. He cupped it, leaned over, and lit the end of the joined cords. As he did, he heard Crake just behind him and turned, throwing himself at him. The two intertwined men fell back toward the shoreline. Faces almost touching, Twomey gagged at the stench of Crake's breath but held on. His body bucked with agonizing pain and a scream escaped his raw throat when Crake sliced into his stomach with the chisel, but he kept his arms around Crake.

The light in the cave was dimming, along with the throbbing, and his mother's voice returned. Not a lullaby this time, but a summoning call.

He couldn't feel his legs anymore. His arms still worked, though, and he tightened his grip around Crake's waist as the other jerked and twisted the chisel, creating a gouge large enough that intestines began sliding out.

The two were still locked together when the crackling flame completed its journey down the shorter length of cord and the cavern entrance collapsed.

Daniel didn't hear the explosion when the second, longer fuse set off the explosives at the outer mine entrance, nor the cries of rage from what had formerly been Lottie Crake.

He was following the sound of his mother's voice, welcoming him home.

Chapter 12

Following the resealing of the cavern, the *Fomórach* had spent
a decade in righteous anger at the pitiful creatures keeping it
from its rightful place in the world but as its anger cooled,
it considered. Yes, some of the human cattle had retained the
ability to fight off its power and, although it didn't enjoy the
admission, it had underestimated them. But as a race, they had
lost any knowledge of the lore that could truly defeat it. It need
only wait for another opportunity. It had lived for thousands
of human generations and could be patient. Another chance
would come.

And that chance was now here.

When Tierney completed his check of the Rathcrooghan, he
received a tingling approval. He walked to a boulder near

the cavern entrance, desiccated bodies of the cavern's last occupants piled behind it.

Francis Gill's great-granddaughter lay on her back, wrists and ankles tied with thick, coarse rope attached to lengths of metal rebar driven deep into the stony ground.

She looked back, wordlessly, as he dug his fingers into a wide gash in her leg and, pulling them out, sucked the red dripping blood from them.

The screams from Fran Hopper echoed through the chamber, but Dennis Tierney paid no attention. He mentally acknowledged the unspoken message that the police chief must be alive for the ceremony, licked his fingers, and went to see to the final arrangements. Time as humans gauged it was meaningless to the *Fomórach*, but there were certain hours when the powers of the earth were more focused than others, and which made certain magiks easier. When the sun had just lifted itself above the horizon was one such time, the remnants of dark power mixing with those of the light before brightness burned it away until the following evening.

And that time was quickly approaching.

The limping Stríocálaí had been guarding the outer entrance to the tunnel, but he knew she was now making her way into the cavern. He faced the cave opening and his thoughts turned to the *Fuilier* and *Acair*. As he did, the two appeared at his side.

The *Fuilier* keened, head bowed, its inscriptions crusted over.

He put his hand under its chin and said gently, "There isn't time, little one, but you will soon be more than fulfilled."

To the *Acair*, he said, "Take your position."

From her bound vantage on top of the boulder, Fran Hopper watched as Carl Miller moved to stand beside the rectangular framework.

Rathcrooghan, she thought.

To her core, she was a pragmatic woman. She had enlisted after getting a philosophy degree, not being content with esoteric and inscrutable non-answers, and wanting to make a difference in the real world. That same urge had driven her to enter the police academy when her second hitch was over.

Granted, the horrors and sadness she had seen in the Army were not exclusive to Afghanistan, but at least in Prescott, they were the exception, not the rule.

And what she saw and experienced as she rose through the ranks of the police force was understandable, pinned to reality, however heart-breaking it might be. Unlike one supply run made during her second hitch...

Let's not think about that right now, shall we?

Her belief or disbelief in a god or, for that matter, a devil, was not relevant to the current situation. She may not understand the metaphysical aspects of what was going on, but she did understand people had died and more might, very much including her. She concentrated on what was happening around her to determine what options she might have.

The blow to the head had dazed her, but she hadn't passed out, so knew not much time had passed since she had been dragged here and Holly had escaped.

Holly.

The state troopers' tactical team should arrive in Prescott within the hour, checking in at the station to coordinate before heading out to Warner. Holly, assuming she made it back to the cruiser, could warn them about the traps and Tierney.

Drilling through the pain in her leg and head, she considered. Holly was smart enough to know the right thing to do was to either wait at the car for backup with Bob and Clarence or drive back to Prescott and meet the tactical team in person.

Smart enough, yes, but she wears her heart on her sleeve, just like you did before Kandahar.

She knew the dispatcher had a crush on her, whatever denials she made. The fact was, Hopper found the younger woman attractive. Smart, fun...and totally off-limits. She was, first, last, and at all points in between, her superior.

But she worried that Holly would feel driven to try some sort of rescue without waiting for help, thinking it might be too long in coming.

If so, she was probably right about backup being too late to help Hopper. But she did not want the dispatcher attempting any sort of kamikaze run at Tierney. The younger woman might have guts and gotten top points in marksmanship at the Academy, but she was still so wet behind the ears she dripped, and had no real field experience. Fran had planned on working with her over time, having seen the potential there, but that had yet to happen.

And, she admitted, at this point it probably wouldn't.

Unless she could get out of the current situation, she chastised herself, and before the other woman got herself killed.

Her eyes remained on Miller as these thoughts ran through her mind, and she now saw the old man struggle to undo his pants after removing his shirt. His crippled hands finally managed to unclip the baggy trousers, and they dropped to his feet. He pulled his soiled underwear down as well and stepped out of both, kicking them to the side.

Tierney walked back to her. Pamela positioned herself across the boulder at Fran's left.

"Whatever you're doing, Tierney, you–"Hopper interrupted herself with another scream as he poked a finger into the open wound on her leg. He did not, however, partake of another snack.

"Hush now," he said. "You should be honored for your part in all of this."

Fran Hopper's teeth ground together as she tried to force the pain away, pushing it into a sealed container in her mind, separate from herself. She needed to be as clear-headed as possible if there was any opportunity that gave her even a slight chance of changing the odds.

Tierney pulled her Glock from his belt and pushed it against her neck. He used his other hand to pull on the knot securing her foot to the metal bar in the ground; Hotchkins did the same on her other side. When they were free, the two worked on the ropes tying her arms down, the dentist showing no concern when she winced at the tugging on her damaged wrist.

Knowing it was unlikely to accomplish anything, but short on ideas at the moment, Hopper turned her head toward the Chamber president and said, "Pamela, think about—"

The gun moved away from her throat and glanced lightly off her head, dazing her. She saw a bright flash of light when the gun made contact and blinked before turning back to face the dentist.

"Now, now, Miss Hopper. You need to remain more or less intact and conscious, but that doesn't mean a concussion is out of the question."

He was smiling at her, and she saw his teeth, too many and jagged, ending in wicked looking points.

A chill ran through her.

Her arms untied now, he brought the gun back up, this time pointing it at her face from a distance of a few inches.

He motioned for her to get up.

Holly made it back to the forest's edge where Clarence and Bob waited, sprinting the entire way. As she approached the tree line, she called out.

"It's Holly! Stand down!"

She tripped as she entered the scrub brush and hit face first.

"Nice, Holly," Clarence said, stepping out from behind a sycamore. Bob appeared from a dozen yards to the right, watching the path Holly had followed.

"Cut the shit, Clarence," Bob said. "You ok, Holly? Where's the Chief?"

"Shit!" She stood, brushing herself off. "I am, but we have to get back in there. Larry is dead and—"

"'the fuck?" Bob exclaimed as Clarence said, "What–"

"Shut up, Bob." The viciousness of the comment brought immediate silence from both men who stared at her. "It was an ambush. He's dead, and they captured the Chief." She was still grappling with what she had seen. "Carl Miller and Meredith Baxter are working with Tierney and Pamela Hotchkins."

The men continued to look at her, not really comprehending.

Their responses overlapped.

"That doesn't make any sense."

"The tactical team will—"

She snapped, "The tactical team will be here too late to do a fucking thing, Bob. Considering they put a piece of rebar through Larry's God damn head, I don't think the Chief has a lot of time to spare, do you?"

Dead silence again.

She knew it wasn't fair to spew venom at the two of them, but she was reeling from the night's events. Bob asked quietly, "What's the plan, then?"

She started to snap again, then saw the look on their two faces.

She was a goddamn dispatcher. But looking at Bob and Clarence, she realized their entire careers had been as Prescott cops. A lot of domestic violence calls, even more animal nuisance calls, with far too many ODs mixed in. Violence wasn't unheard of by any stretch in Prescott, any more than it was in any small town, but the depth of what was going on was so foreign to them that their instinct was to turn to someone in charge for direction.

And there wasn't anyone left in charge at this point. There was only her.

She took a silent, deep breath.

"All right. First, I'm going to get hold of Callie, get an updated ETA on the tac team and also have her requisition some ATVs to be brought in with them. We'll have tac come directly in, then…"

She had no actual plan when she began speaking, but as she continued, trying to project the calmness and certainty Fran Hopper always managed to, no matter the situation, an idea formed. By the time she finished outlining what she had in mind, she thought it had a chance of working.

"Seems dicey."

Well, I didn't say it was a good chance.

She responded to Clarence, "Maybe so, but unless one of you has a better idea, it's our best shot at getting the Chief out of there and, with any luck, shutting Tierney down." She looked at them.

After sharing a look with his partner, Bob said, "Ok, Holly. It's worth a shot."

She nodded at them and said, "Let's get to it."

Chapter 13

There had been no opportunity to attempt a getaway, or anything else, as they escorted her, hobbling, to the grotesque framework. Although it was only twenty feet or so from the boulder to the skin doorway, she had almost fallen twice, her leg having a hard time supporting her. When Tierney put his arm under her shoulders to assist in a companionably way, her entire being was revulsed even before the death-stink hit her. She would have vomited if she hadn't forced herself to remember she couldn't afford to lose focus for even a moment.

There were four more pieces of rebar hammered into the ground a yard in front of the skin-frame, the water from the glowing lake held in abeyance behind it by a large stone.

As if he were assisting a date into a dining chair at an upscale restaurant, Tierney waved toward the ground with the gun in his free hand, tilting his head down in a mini bow, then lowered her carefully to the ground. Pamela Hotchkins, who had accompanied them on their short walk, had said nothing to this point, but now grunted as she took Fran's other arm and assisted.

She had an absurd impulse to say thank you, but stifled her innate politeness as she sat on the rubble. Her seat was next to a long narrow furrow running from the frame to a slightly lower opening in the cave wall, that opening also blocked by a large rock.

She realized she didn't have much time left. Unfortunately, between the gun in Tierney's hand, her throbbing leg, and a most-likely broken wrist, her options were limited. Then she remembered that whatever the plan was, the demented dentist had said she had to be intact for whatever it was.

Her eyes moved quickly between Hotchkins and Tierney as the man said, "Scooch around, please." He indicated for her to lie across the ditch.

She complied, exaggerating the damage to her leg, not that it needed much exaggeration, using her good hand to move it. At the delay, Tierney gestured to Hotchkins, who bent over and began helping her turn her body around. Fran's left hand shot out, extended fingers together, hard against her thumb, and rammed it into the base of the other woman's throat, rolling as she did.

The pain in her leg was immediate and was quickly followed by a screaming agony in her wrist as it got caught under her during the roll.

But she completed the semi-somersault, ending up next to Hotchkins, who was still clutching her throat. The policewoman's good hand reached out again and grabbed the stunned woman's throat. A brief thrashing subsided quickly when she squeezed harder.

She glared up at Tierney.

"Oh my, that was impressive."

Hopper's nostrils flared as she forced down the pain and tried to catch her breath.

The former dentist continued to study her, cocking his head.

"You know I can't let you leave. Nor," he waved the gun absently at the gasping half-naked woman in her grasp, "can I allow you to harm her."

Breath coming steadier now, she responded, "I think you better rethink that."

Sharp-edged teeth surround by blackened gums shone once again as a sound… vibration…both…hit her brain and entire body, growing to a blare.

Her hand loosened its grip on Hotchkin's throat, but at the first movement from her captive, she tightened it again, shaking her head to clear it.

The white noise continued to increase, and she felt her nerves oscillating under her skin. She called back to the lessons she had learned under Myung Jung-Soo, her first Hapkido

Master, when she began studying the discipline as a teenager. She slowed her breathing even more, and focused on the internal image of a small ball of light as she built a wall, brick by brick, around it. As brick stacked upon brick, her eyes never left Tierney's grinning face, nor did her hand relax from around the pulsing throat of Pamela Hotchkins.

She couldn't cancel the throbbing entirely, but it receded enough that she was able to return the deformed smile with one of her own. As she did, the man's predatory grin dimmed.

"What else you got?" She didn't quite have to force the words out, but she was hanging on tightly to avoid being overwhelmed by whatever it was trying to drill into her head. She suspected if she faltered, she would end up in similar, or worse, shape than Miller and Hotchkins.

To her surprise, the dentist threw his head back and laughed. If she had heard it under any other circumstances, she would have thought whoever came out with it had just heard the best joke of their life.

She didn't allow herself to be distracted, however. She watched him as he gasped a bit, the laughter finally tapering off. When he spoke again, it was in two simultaneous tones. It seemed she was now speaking to more than the transplanted dentist.

"I am *quite* impressed, Officer Hopper. I knew there remained a streak of stubbornness in your kind, but I hadn't realized quite how deep yours was."

Her eyes slitted.

"What are you?"

"More than you could possibly imagine."

"Well, that tells me shit-all."

A chuckle this time.

"My apologies, but it is time." Tierney's eyes gestured over her head, and something hit Hopper from behind. Her hand came free from Pamela Hotchkins' throat as she was thrown forward and tumbled over, hitting her broken wrist again as she did.

Her vision clouded with a purple and black haze. When it cleared, Meredith Baxter, Pamela Hotchkins, and Dennis Tierney stood in a semi-circle around her, the latter with her sidearm pointed at her face. She could see over Pamela's shoulder that Carl Miller's naked form had not moved from his spot next to the Rathcrooghan.

Panting, she gritted out, "You said I have to be intact."

He adjusted his aim to her injured leg and squeezed the trigger.

Her kneecap shattered.

She rolled onto her side, unable to think through the pain. She didn't hear his next comment.

"My apologies. I should have said, 'alive'."

Arms lifted her and dragged her agony-ridden body back to the spikes set up by the shallow gulley. She gave no protest in either word or action as her captors gathered the ropes from the boulder and tied her to the rebar, her back nestled in the furrow.

She tried to focus, but the bricks tumbled, and the ball of light kept bursting into a nova. Slowly, so slowly, she came back to awareness of her surroundings, but there was no easement for her tortured body.

Baxter was just visible past the framework, apparently laying across the stones. Miller continued his silent sentinelling and Hotchkins was now in front of the stitched skin, her clothing also discarded.

Her Glock was back in Tierney's waistband, a machete-sized knife in one hand.

As she continued to focus on her breathing and compartmentalizing the pain, Tierney sketched a line through the stones, starting on the right side of the gateway. It arced around Hotchkins, across the ditch, around Miller, and back to the lip of luminescent water. His mouth formed sounds as he made the path, although she didn't hear any words.

When he had completed his circuit, he stopped next to the once-respected insurance agency owner and leaned close to

Miller's head. Lips still moving, she could see Carl's face light up in a smile.

The knife thrust forward, entering just above the old man's waist, and continued until the steel gray tip emerged out the other side. His expression didn't change as blood seeped out around the hilt of the blade.

Tierney's hand came up and grasped Carl by the back of the neck, tilting his limp body over the channel leading toward her and the cavern wall. He pulled the knife free, and blood began pouring in a slow stream into the hollowed-out channel. After a few seconds, he pulled Carl back. She caught a glimpse of his glassy eyes as he was turned and tipped forward over the lake now. The blade came up and in a smooth motion ran across his throat, his carotid artery spouting bright red and raining into the glowing water.

The muttering from Tierney was just audible now.

Mar a chaidh aithris ann an sgrìobhaidhean Craghnoth, gabh ris an ìobairt as lugha de do chruthachaidhean, màthair nan uile.

Çatalhöy, tha an t-seile air a losgadh agus tha na h-ullachaidhean faisg air deireadh. Bidh an talamh a 'ruith dearg leis an fhiadh-bheathaich fala, thèid do shlighe a ghlanadh agus slaodadh le inntinn nan ainmhidhean.

Thoir foirm mo chorp a-rithist.

While she did not know what the words meant, her great-grandfather, raised before English overlords made the teaching or even speaking of Irish illegal, would have understood.

It was a supplication. To a creature forgotten by mankind over one hundred fifty generations before, faded even from legend, except for fragments passed down through fairy tales.

A supplication, and a summoning of power.

This time, the white noise wasn't in her head but emanating from the walls of the cave itself. The lake shone even brighter, and Dennis Tierney discarded the husk of Carl Miller, his body dropping to the stones with a thud. Tierney stepped to straddle the channel, standing behind Pamela Hotchkins.

Hopper saw a new glow coming from the erstwhile mayor as Tierney's voice rose in volume. She would not have called the sounds he was making words, nor would she have even imagined human vocal cords could make the sounds.

As he continued, a shimmering filled the cavern. The surface of the water, the cave walls, even Tierney and the others all seemed to be shifting into and out of sync with reality.

She tried pulling on the rope, holding her uninjured arm with no more success than she had had a few minutes before. Nausea continued to hit her in waves, and she didn't allow herself to think about her destroyed knee. Instead, she began flipping through ideas that might allow her to extricate herself from this hellscape.

None were remotely feasible in the current situation.

As she continued grasping at mental straws, Tierney's monotone, guttural syllables filled the chamber.

Suddenly, Pamela's body stiffened, her outline just visible around Tierney. The discordant noises from the dentist ceased, and his head began moving in some sort of pattern behind Hotchkins as he bent and stood straight again. The movement continued for a short while, then he stepped away from Hotchkins.

She could see his profile now. It was not the profile of the man she had known in passing on the streets of Prescott, nor even that of the cheerfully demented, murderous predator of a short time ago. His lower jaw hung down half a foot below his upper, the skin connecting the two stretched to shininess, seeping bloody tears around the edges of his mouth.

In horror, Fran looked at the second mouth extended outward on blackened tissue from his human mouth. The second showed the outline of the bones supporting it under streaked flesh and it opened and closed with a smacking sound, rows of multiple pointed teeth clacking together.

Her gaze snapped to Pamela Hotchkins' naked back, and she saw deep, ugly marks running in rows up and down the woman's torso. The flesh was covered in blood, but even through the gore, she could make out what appeared to be rows of characters in some unknown script.

She dry-heaved and fought to regain a semblance of her slipping sanity.

Tierney turned fully to her, and the second mouth spoke, or so she assumed. As before, whatever sounds that came from it were not anything any human had ever uttered.

After a moment, muscles contracted, and the second mouth pulled itself back into Dennis Tierney's mouth, disappearing from view. The man swallowed, as though clearing his throat, and smiled at her again.

The shark-grin was almost a relief.

She expected him to continue speaking to her, perhaps this time in English, but he looked away instead toward Meredith Baxter, whose face had remained serene throughout the proceedings.

Baxter turned her head toward Tierney and, in response to an unasked question, said in a little-girl's voice, "Yes, please."

He nodded and lifted the knife, congealed blood coating its length.

Chapter 14

If rescue plans were an Olympic event, Holly was sure this one would be rated "impossible difficulty". She only hoped the judges, and God, would be more kind when it came to execution.

She had been on the knife-edge of paranoia when they first entered the tunnel, more than half expecting the ground to erupt again and Carl or one of the others, or maybe Bigfoot, to jump out and take them down. After what had already occurred, nothing would surprise her.

But they had made it to the small side tunnel with no issues. The two men froze when they saw Larry's body lying in the main tunnel, rebar sticking out his mouth, face frozen in an eternal grin. She nudged them and they all stepped into the anteroom, wiping fear-tainted sweat from their faces. She pulled their heads to hers, foreheads touching, as she confirmed the next steps in her plan in whispers.

The two were still there in the side tunnel, assuming they hadn't bolted the moment she stepped out and began creeping down the main tunnel.

In football parlance, it was a Hail Mary play, a last-ditch effort to pull victory from a pending ash heap. She had never been interested in the sport, but at Jenkins High unless you had a reasonable excuse not to attend a game, say the death of a parent or a car crash that put you in a coma, you either went to all the home games or you could spend the time until graduation doing an imitation of a desert island castaway. She hadn't come out regarding her sexuality until college, so had attended all the games in her efforts to fit in.

The likelihood, she knew, of not only living through to the completion of her plan but actually rescuing the Chief was remote, forget about capturing Tierney or any of the others.

But it didn't matter.

She had heard many stories about what happened to the Chief in Afghanistan, most conflicting. What they all seemed to agree upon, though, was that Hopper's eighteen (or maybe twenty) vehicle supply convoy, accompanied by thirty-two (or perhaps fifty-two) personnel under her command, had driven into an ambush. Hopper was riding shotgun in the second vehicle when the driver slumped down following the first volley of gunfire and the lead truck hit an IED, an improvised explosive device. A number of trucks were destroyed and over a dozen people were killed in the first few minutes of the firefight that followed the initial detonation. Hopper consolidated her people's position around the remaining vehicles, called in air support, and gotten all her remaining unit, as well as the bodies of their fallen comrades, out.

The stories got improbable from there. Some had her leading a charge into an insurgent's gunner's nest, personally taking out two, or three, or a dozen, of the attackers. In other versions, she had done it single-handedly and unarmed, having been trained by ninjas.

And those were the most plausible of the ones she had heard.

But whether her Chief was a ninja, a warrior princess, or none of the above didn't matter. Holly had seen Fran Hopper in action and knew that Hopper didn't leave her people behind and that she didn't give up.

So neither would she.

Inching down the tunnel toward the brightly lit cavern opening, she could feel, and smell, her sweat-soaked shirt as it rubbed against the rough wall surface. A Colt rifle obtained from another trip back to the squad car was up against her chest, her right hand over the trigger guard, index finger just above the trigger. Her sidearm was in its holster which was unsnapped. Unfortunately, Bob and Clarence had only their revolvers.

Part of her wished she and the other officers had more armament, but she realized that realistically, it was going to come down to a surprise advantage and a shitload of luck breaking their way.

Just ahead, the stone path inclined slightly upward, plateauing at an opening about five feet high. She leaned out from the wall carefully, blinking her eyes to accustom them to the brighter light. Through the cleared entryway, she could make out a large body of water that appeared to be phosphorescent.

There.

At the closest edge of the water stood Tierney, Pamela Hotchkins, and Carl, near some sort of free-standing rectangle made up of plastic pipes. The center was...

She swallowed and raised the rifle to her eye, looking through the night scope to, hopefully, contradict what she thought she saw.

No, it is what I thought it was.

Some of the center covering of the frame was sun-darkened, some pale, some as dark as the Chief's own skin. Portions were smooth, others covered in varying short lengths and hues of hair.

She almost dropped the weapon, but pulled it back to her chest and leaned against the wall, drawing deep breaths through her nose. She closed her eyes, opened them again, and leaned back out.

On the ground opposite the frame from the Chief lay Meredith Baxter, seemingly unconcerned by anything around her. The waitress might as well have been sunning herself at the beach.

As she watched, Tierney began drawing in the stones with the machete in his hands, moving around the structure as he did. When he got to Carl Miller, she swallowed a gasp as he stabbed the old man. After leaning him forward over the ditch running from the structure, he tipped Carl over the water and slit his throat, blood pouring down into the partially obscured lake.

Oh, Carl…I am so sorry.

Her thoughts were not for the deranged, mutilated man that had taken part in the tunnel killing. It was for the smiling, impish gent she had shared drinks and personal stories with at the bar a lifetime ago.

Her hand reached up toward her personal radio but paused as she saw Tierney step behind Pamela Hotchkins, and reality skewed five degrees further off kilter.

What the hell?

The entire cavern and its occupants seemed to double, a fuzzy, overlapped version of everything merging into and out of the actual cave and people. She glanced down at herself and saw nothing had changed but looking back to where the Chief lay spread-eagle, the strange image-convergence repeated, again and again, including of Hopper.

Tierney was speaking, although she couldn't make out what he was saying. And she saw that now the preternatural light of the water had been joined by a glow coming from around Hotchkins.

Tierney's voice ceased. He turned, and his face became fully visible.

She fought a scream. One hand came up from the rifle and covered her mouth, trying to stifle the cry that fought to escape.

He isn't human. That mouth...

She had looked away from him, her own mouth filled with saliva, trying not to throw up, but her gaze latched onto Pamela Hotchkins' back.

Vomit spilled through her hand, and she crouched back against the wall, head bent, rifle to the side, as the last of the earlier wine splashed onto the stones.

Thank God the Chief didn't see that, came the ludicrous thought, but it snapped her back and she wiped slime from her mouth, straightening and looking out at the hellish scene again.

The dentist was now at the head-end of the Chief and Baxter, the horror of a second mouth somehow gone. As he raised the machete again, she knew there was no more time and reached up, clicking her radio transmit button three times in rapid sequence. One more deep breath and she semi-crouched, putting most of her weight on her back leg, then leaped forward, running toward and up the short incline.

The Fomórach *was balancing between power and constraint. The pain and blood of the earlier sacrifices had filled it with energy, yet it knew it had to marshal its reserves until the ceremony was complete. It needed immense power to recreate its physical form, and the entirety of its being and focus had to remain on the progression of the final stages of the ritual. Even the vitality it had used to penetrate and punish the dark-skinned female was a loss, although it did not regret the act. There was something familiar about the scent of her intractable life-force that had driven it to lash out.*

But no matter. Her blood would act as a coda to the ceremony, re-invigorating the small piece of itself it must leave behind in the water. When the channel was opened and poured down and into the feeder stream for the Prescott's drinking supply, the humans would take their rightful place as its pliant cattle, to be dressed and butchered as it wished.

The sustenance it took via its vessels, through their own or inflicted pain, only made it more ravenous; it looked forward to once again being able to rend fresh meat from bone with its own claws, devouring the flesh and cracking the marrow from what remained.

When the Acair's *blood dripped into the water, it felt a surge and urged its primary vessel on to the next stage. As the* Scribner *read the inscription from the flesh of the* Fuilier, *then carved the proper response into it, the* Fomórach *could feel the wall thinning around its prison.*

The Scribner *now stood over the* Stríocálaí.

Through the eyes of its primary vessel, it watched the blade come up, preparing to saturate the channel with the lesser vessel's vital fluid when a high-pitched wheet! cut through vibrating air and the Scribner was knocked to the ground.

All things considered, it was a pretty damn good shot. Holly hadn't been certain how much time she would have when she scrambled down stones into the cavern, but her presence appeared to be unnoticed as she brought the rifle up. She sighted on the center of Tierney's chest, hoping the unadjusted scope was close enough to true that she would at least startle, if not wing, him and stop the blade from its descent.

She had never shot a human being before and had wondered during training, and since, how she would react if she made full officer and ran into a scenario where it was required. Thankfully, she had not hesitated.

The shot hit Tierney high and right of where she had aimed, just below the left shoulder. She watched him jerk backwards, dropping the machete as he fell. A moment later, his body thrashed side to side, and he pushed himself upright before standing again, picking up the blade as he did.

It was then she realized she still hadn't shot a human being.

Tierney, or whatever he was now, looked toward her calmly. There was a growing dark red stain on his already mottled shirt. The air in the cavern, shimmering and vibrating, seemed to thicken and her head took a hit from something she couldn't see but felt down to her police-issue work boots.

She swung the Colt to block whatever had struck her, but there was nothing there. The ache in her head grew, but she re-focused on Tierney.

He raised the blade again and did something that would have garnered her a shellacking from both her father and the instructors at the Academy - she aimed the rifle from her hip and squeezed off a shot.

It grazed his right side, enough to make him sway back a bit and pause his downward swing.

She and Fran were out of time, and she knew it. She dropped the rifle and sprinted forward, wondering where the *hell* Bob and Clarence were.

There was a cry behind her. It may have earned nothing more than disdain from his ancient forebears if they had heard it, but Clarence Edwards, a boy raised in the hollers of rural West Virginia, did justice to the gravelly call that fans of the Prescott Wildcats had given for his high school football team.

She didn't turn when the yell rang through the cave, but her lip curled slightly as she covered the remaining distance to her injured Chief. That slight smile disappeared when a shot from one of the two men behind her whipped by so close a lock of pink-streaked hair was sliced away, but she kept going and offered a silent prayer that their aim would quickly improve.

When she had laid out the plan to Bob and Clarence, she had assumed Tierney would try to take shelter, either behind whatever stones must dot the cavern or perhaps using one of the people as a human shield. If the latter, all she could hope for was that it wouldn't be Fran Hopper.

But that assumption had been when she had still believed him to be human.

Rather than look for refuge, he seemed to brace himself as multiple rounds from Bob and Clarence tore through his body and he smiled at them.

Oh, shit.

The smile and mouth continued extending. When the second mouth appeared, the shots from behind her stopped.

She turned and saw her backup frozen in their tracks. Not that she could blame them, but there wasn't time.

"Keep moving!"

There was as much gravel and *no questions* tone in her words as she could manage, and she was gratified to see them start forward again after a quick glance in her direction.

She turned back toward the unfolding scene and began running again.

Until she closed in on Hopper, she hadn't realized how badly injured her Chief's leg was.

How the hell is she still conscious?

"I told you to get out."

She bit back a retort when she saw the strained smile on the Chief's face.

"Write me up when we get back to the station."

She pulled a utility knife from her belt and began sawing through the thick ropes holding Hopper down. There was more gunfire, and she looked up after freeing Hopper's hands. Bob was a few yards from Tierney, gun straight out and still firing, while Clarence had cut slightly to the side and had stopped by Meredith Baxter's feet.

His gun hand came down.

"Clarence, what are you doing?" Bob shouted. His gun *clicked*.

Clarence Edwards spun around and brought the Glock back up, this time directed toward his partner.

"Clarence, for fuck's–"

The bullet entered his stomach and cut him off, then shattered his spine as it exited through his back.

Bob went down.

She crawled to Hopper's feet and sawed through the rope holding Hopper's injured leg. A bullet scattered stones by the prone woman's feet, and she looked up to see Clarence swing his aim toward them.

Fran gritted out, "I think you best hurry, Holly. Good news is Tierney said it's against the rules for them to kill me."

The frayed rope came free, and she reached over her boss's legs, hoping Hopper was right and not giving any thought to her own position as she sawed at the braids holding the other ankle.

A grunt of pain and she saw another shot had glanced off the Chief's thigh.

"Fran, I–"

"Said they wouldn't kill me. Didn't say they wouldn't poke more holes in me or kill you. Hurry up. Please."

She ducked her head down behind Fran's calf and kept cutting until the rope dropped apart.

Another bullet ricocheted off the stones, just short of Hopper's leg.

She pulled herself into a squat and dove forward, rolling over the top of Hopper's legs. As she came up, she slid the Glock from its holster, not even trying to aim.

Clarence dropped heavily to the stones, the round having caught him in the chest.

As she stood, Tierney stepped forward, hell-mouth clicking open and closed.

She called out, "I'll cover you, Fran. Find cover in one of the buildings until the troopers get here," and started firing.

Rounds whistled past Tierney's head until one carried off a chunk of his scalp with it. Another followed that bullet and severed part of an ear. A few more missed shots and she aimed lower, watching as three rounds shattered his chest just below her earlier shot.

The Tierney-creature turned back toward Meredith Baxter and brought the machete down, splitting Baxter's face and lodging the blade in her skull.

Holly thought she saw an expression of relief on the remains of Meredith's mangled face before it was blotted out by Tierney's boot when he braced himself and yanked the machete free.

There was a click when she squeezed the trigger again, and she had a mental flash of the rifle still lying on the ground somewhere behind her.

She holstered the pistol and strode forward toward something even her worst nightmares had never conjured.

CHAPTER 15

The Fuilier *stood in front of him as the* Scribner *murmured phrases that had not been spoken on this plane since man's ancestors lived in trees. The second extended mouth added vibratory counterpoint to the human speech.*

With each word uttered, the inscribed skin of the Fuilier *shifted; swells in the ingrained flesh undulated. She removed her pants and pressed up against the* Scribner *as he tore at his own clothing.*

Their two bodies pressed against each other and the Fomórach's *essence reached out, both vessels' flesh pushing outward. The air itself oscillated as the rippling quickened and the vessels' faces began distending.*

There was a popping sound and the light that had emanated from Pamela Hotchkins' former body burst into a flaming orange, filling the cavern.

Holly thought she might pay a visit to Morgantown First Methodist if she lived through this, but realized it was more unlikely than ever she would leave the cavern alive. One thing she was certain of, however, was that she would not allow herself, or Fran, to become whatever Tierney and the former inn keeper-mayor had become...were becoming.

She panted to catch her breath. The air, which was heavy in her lungs, seemed to flow in waves around the cave.

There was a flash, and she was knocked back on her ass, temporarily blinded as Hotchkins appeared to catch fire.

Rubbing her eyes, first to clear the afterimage, then to bring sense to the scene, she saw Hotchkins had not, in fact, gone up in flames. Rather, the fiery colors swirled around both Tierney's and her naked forms. The glow was so bright it brought the entire cave into dim relief.

The two bodies clutched each other, and she saw Tierney had an erection that a porn star would give a year's salary for. Thick strands of blackish drool dripped down from the extended second mouth.

Hotchkins pulled herself up onto the murderous dentist, arms wrapped around his neck, and threw back her head. She screamed as she lowered herself onto his pulsating shaft.

Tierney's two mouths continued moving, although Holly couldn't hear anything. The light intensified and hovered around the figures, and she saw Tierney's fingers thicken and elongate into curved claws, which dug into Hotchkins' back. Both his and Hotchkins' skin stretched out from their bodies, meeting and somehow merging. He stepped heavily forward toward the grisly framework, carrying Hotchkins in a perverse reverse piggy-back. The woman moved up and down on him, her cries of ecstasy continuing as he stopped by the skin-frame.

Dual tones joined the twisted note of rapture, double mouths now howling.

One after another, the strands holding the horrific vellum to the frame snapped. As they did, the patchwork of skin floated toward Tierney and Hotchkins, moving through the brilliant glare as though it wasn't there. It wrapped itself around them, rippling as their own flesh had been. They were quickly cocooned, but the outlines of their bodies shone through the flesh covering.

Holly saw what was happening, pushed herself up and rushed forward, only to be repelled just outside the cone of orange light that surrounded the two.

The light wasn't a wall so much as an elasticity that met her blows with a flex inward, which inexorably pushed back into its original shape. She picked up a rock, trying to pierce it, slam through it, anything.

She thought of Fran briefly, and hoped she was making her way, however painfully, out the entrance to the cavern. There was no thought of leaving. Whatever was happening within that envelope meant death for the people of Prescott and, perhaps, beyond. It had to be stopped before it got out of the cave.

She continued beating against the light envelope with no success. There were voices beneath the skin that she could feel more than hear and she gasped, trying to get enough oxygen as the air continued to thicken.

She jumped when she felt something touch her shoulder. Rock still in hand, she whirled and saw Fran Hopper leaning heavily on the rifle Holly had dropped.

"Chief! Why aren't you gone?" She couldn't help the feeling of elation, however, at the other woman's presence.

"Couldn't let a mere dispatcher have all the fun," Hopper responded. "And I think under the circumstances, Fran works better than Chief, don't you?" The lightness of her words contrasted with her gray pallor. Holly wasn't about to argue, although she realized Fran had signed her own death warrant.

"Any ideas?" she asked Hopper. The stretching and pulling within the skin just a few feet away had increased. To her surprise, Fran held out the rifle, leaning back on her good leg.

"Shoot them."

She paused for a moment, feeling nonplussed.

Jesus, why not?

She took the weapon from Fran, noticing a slight tremor in the outstretched hand, pulled the magazine to check it, slammed it back in place, and focused through the light cone on the center of the cocoon.

The three rounds she let off in quick succession pierced the colors barrier, sparks flying in their wake. There seemed to be a single silhouette inside the skin wrapping now, one side slightly higher than the other. As the bullets made impact with it, the shape straightened, but there was no other visible reaction.

She brought the rifle back into position and fired round after round until the large capacity magazine was spent. Most of the bullets, she was certain, had hit their intended targets, but they didn't seem to have done any damage. She had turned back to Fran when she heard a tearing sound behind her and spun back.

The cocoon was opening, top down, but the tearing sound wasn't limited to the envelope around Tierney and Hotchkins. The entire cavern reverberated with the noise and the stones underfoot began vibrating as the walls surrounding the water ebbed into and out of focus again.

"Hold your breath!"

She jerked toward Fran, who was pointing at the lake. The water had receded from its banks, rising in the center as the additional water added to the existing volume. It was at twice Hopper's height and swung back and forth like a cobra preparing to strike an unobservant rodent.

It coalesced into a spearpoint and, faster than she thought possible, shot toward them.

She took a quick breath and closed her mouth as the water, luminescent as the glow around Tierney and Hotchkins, slammed into the two women, splashing down and around them. Her arm reached out protectively to grab Hopper's.

She wiped her face off, and spit to clear her mouth of the bit of liquid that had gotten in. Hopper looked at her with concern, but she waved back reassuringly. Fran, too, was soaked, but appeared to be intact, thankfully.

The tearing of the cocoon had continued during the watery onslaught and the opening, now a few inches wide, ran from the top of the leathery-looking covering to the ground.

Her glimpse inside told her it was no longer either Tierney or Hotchkins.

She squeezed Hopper's arm and said, "We have to get out of here."

Fran Hopper had also been staring at the tear and nodded silently.

She slid her arm around Fran and they semi-staggered toward the hole back to the main tunnel.

The ripping sound grew, but she didn't look back.

She did, however, quicken her pace slightly, mentally urging the other woman on, not wanting to do more damage to Fran's leg.

To the cacophony of the cocoon, a loud crackling was now added, and razor thin beams of light shot from the cavern walls and ceiling.

They reached the bottom of the incline, and Hopper grabbed her arm, leaning and pushing herself heavily up.

She finally chanced a look back and saw the light around the broken cocoon snap into and out of existence. The tear was now two or three feet wide in the center and large, scaled claws gripped either edge from inside, pushing it further open.

Fran's hand was no longer on her shoulder, and she looked to see the wounded woman leaning against the cavern opening. Fran grunted and said, "Move it, Holly."

She gave a quick nod and scrambled up the stones, dropping the now-useless rifle as she did.

And froze, her brain shot through with a piercing pain.

No...no...stop...

"Holly. Holly!"

Fran...what?

Hopper's face was inches from her own but it, and the words that tried to cut through the haze, were unimportant. She turned back toward the lake.

And saw an angel.

"Holly, are you all right? We need to go. Whatever that is, we need to go *now!*" Fingers dug into her arm, but she swatted the hand away.

Come, little one. All will be well.

"Yes."

"Holly, what the hell is wrong with you?" She was being pulled up the incline. Away from the angel and salvation.

She struggled against the hand and took a step back.

The hand returned, this time pulling her around and away from her path.

Thwaack!

She had not been struck since she was five years old. Even then, it hadn't been across the face. Her cheek burned from the blow, and she raised her own arm, hand in a fist, to return it.

Through a mist she saw a woman, slightly bent and breathing heavily, staring at her.

"Stop that," she said with an annoyed tone, and swung her arm.

The dark-skinned creature facing her blocked the blow with a forearm, twisted and pushed Holly's arm away, and the hand came up again.

Whaap!

Her other cheek flared.

Whack!

Thwaaack!

Two more rattling smacks against her face and the orange haze that had surrounded everything faded. She saw Fran was staring at her, hand pulled back for another strike.

"Fran?"

"Holly, snap out of it! It's messing with your head!"

Fran was peering carefully into her eyes.

She raised her arm to block any potential additional slap.

"I'm here, Fran." Another head shake. "I'm here," she repeated, reassuring herself.

The other woman continued looking at her for a moment, then dipped her chin before turning back toward the opening.

Together, the two made it through the opening, then down the incline where they paused, panting. Even a few feet outside the cavern, the air was much easier to take in.

There was a flare from inside the cavern, orange bathing the tunnel for a dozen paces in front of them.

She grabbed Fran's arm, and they started forward again.

We're actually going to make it.

It didn't solve the not-particularly minor problem of how to keep whatever the hell-the-creature-was back in the cavern from escaping, but she would take her victories where she could get them, no matter how small or temporary they might be.

The glow from behind them had lessened, and the tunnel grew dark. Ahead, though, she saw a different hue of darkness, and knew they were close.

"Stop where you are!"

They halted, and she heard Fran Hopper mutter, "Fuck me."

She looked at Fran in shock. Then started to giggle.

An arched eyebrow turned in her direction.

"Sorry, Fran. It's just, I've never heard you really swear."

The only response was a further raising of the eyebrow and a snort. Hopper turned back toward the voice and called out.

"It's Chief Hopper and another officer. Stand down. We're coming out!"

Although she had been supporting the older woman to this point, she found herself almost dragged forward by Hopper.

Positioned around the entrance were state troopers in riot gear, rifles centered on the two women.

As she and Hopper came within a few paces of the opening, there was another shouted order.

"Halt!"

They did, and two of the four troopers peeled away from their entrance posts, coming forward to pat them down. After frisking Fran and her, one yelled, "All clear!"

Another figure came into the tunnel, blocking the filtering light from the entrance.

"Fran?"

Chief Hopper stood straighter, moving to put more weight on Holly again.

"Jim, that you? Well, hellfire, last I heard, you were heading off to Quantico."

There was a snort, reminding her of Hopper's earlier one. The man stepped toward them, and she could somewhat make out his features. Steady eyes and a face that could have been a bit over or under forty..

"I decided I didn't want to slum." Pause. "What the hell is going on, Fran?" He looked from the Hopper to her.

Fran waved, "Holly Willingham, one of my deputies. Holly, Jim Berger, formerly Sergeant Berger of the seventy-second cavalry troop, fourth squadron, now..." she peered at this uniform and said with some surprise, "*Lieutenant* Berger of the state police." She smiled at him. "Thought you were a working man, Jim."

He said, "Decided to see how the other half lives." He smiled back until his eyes glanced downward, and he saw her leg.

"Jesus, Fran, finally ran into something nastier than you." He turned and called over his shoulder. "Get a medic in here, asap!" He slipped his arm under Hopper's free one and between the two of them, they half-carried Hopper to just outside the cave entrance where her wounded Chief leaned against the hillside.

If the former sergeant and Hopper spoke during the shuffle outside, she missed it. It took a minute, but her mind had caught up on the introduction the Chief had made on her behalf.

Some officers might joke about rank, but not Fran Hopper. She realized she had just received a field promotion to deputy.

Deputy!

Then, *Congratulate yourself later.* She chastised herself and re-focused on the two who were indeed still talking.

"—Damned if I know for sure, Jim, but big problems no matter how you slice it."

"With you involved? I'm shocked," came the deadpan reply. "So, what's the tactical?"

Hopper responded with her own question.

"Did you meet up with the coroner and what's the status of the people I dispatched to the Twisted Kitty?"

The trooper frowned.

"If forensics comes back with the results I think they will for the remains we found on the way in, Marshall Lovell is deceased. He appears to have run into an angry buzz saw. As for your people at the bar, they found a slaughterhouse. After confirming there were no survivors and securing the scene, they met up with us back at your station house. They're still there, waiting for further instructions.

More color drained from Hopper's face at his update, but she nodded and said, "Thanks, Jim".

When she didn't go on, Berger regarded her thoughtfully.

"You still haven't brought me up to speed. Fran. What's really going on?"

Fran Hopper took a deep breath before speaking.

"Like I said, I'm still not certain exactly what we are dealing with, but...Jim?"

Steady eyes looked into steady eyes.

"Yeah, Fran?"

"You remember the run we made to Karz? The dust storm and that girl?"

He studied Hopper and his lips pursed, then looked over the mine entrance past the two women.

"Like that, is it? I've always told myself it was fatigue and tricks of the light."

Hopper grunted, "Sure it was," before adding, "But whatever it actually was, this is much, much worse."

She looked at his profile, then a dark hand reached out to lay on his arm.

A moment of silence and Hopper asked, "You trust me?"

He turned back to her and snorted. "Jesus, Fran. What do you need?"

There was a promise in the question, and she knew that whatever the Chief might ask for, Berger would make damned sure she got it.

What happened in Karz?

Never mind. Add it to the boxful of questions she would like to talk to Fran about when this was over.

Whatever response Hopper was going to make was interrupted by another trooper trotting up, medical bag in hand. She glanced at the trio, spotted Hopper's leg and immediately stepped to her, squatting down as she opened the bag.

"Ma'am, we need to get you to a hospital." She gently pulled back a portion of the tattered pants leg around her shattered knee and looked up at her superior. "Now."

Lieutenant Berger nodded at the medic, then looked at the Chief. "I don't suppose you–"

"Not a chance in hell."

The medic gave an incredulous look and stood, facing Hopper, "You don't understand. I don't know how you're even–"

"Collins, drop it."

The trooper turned to Berger. "But sir, her knee–""I said drop it, Officer Collins."

Collins stared at him, back to Hopper, then to him again, her eyes smoldering.

"Yes, sir."

Hopper looked at the medic with sympathy.

"Officer Collins, I appreciate the concern. As soon as I can, I promise I'll let you cart me off to wherever you need me to go." There was an apology in the statement, and Collins' face smoothed a bit. "In the meantime, I wouldn't argue against some painkillers, if you've got any, and they won't mess with my head."

That got her a small smile in return. Collins leaned over and rummaged for a moment in her black bag. She pulled out a small bottle and a hypodermic.

"Either will help, ma'am. The shot a bit more so, though."

Hopper shuddered and held up her hand. "Needles? Not a chance." A grin as she added, "Those things hurt!"

Chapter 16

Holly urged Hopper to at least let the medic do some basic triage on her leg, in addition to the painkillers.

"Fran, you know you're in rough shape. And I...we need you in as good shape as possible for whatever happens next. Please."

She thought it was the *please* that did it. As on edge as she was, she had kept her voice calm and relatively cool. Hopper didn't look happy, but turned back to Collins, standing with her med kit. At Hopper's nod, the medic started working, giving Holly her own small nod of thanks.

The Chief leaned back against the cave wall as her tattered pants leg was cut away. The ashen woman stared at Holly, who fought to not look away and keep her own gaze steady. After a moment, Fran's lip curled up in the semblance of a smile.

"So, what next, Deputy Hollingsworth?"

"I, ah, was sort of hoping you had some ideas, Chief."

Hopper chuckled, but it turned into a quick sucking sound as Collins began wrapping a bandage around her knee.

Through gritted teeth, Hopper said, "Oh, I do." She glanced down at the medic. "Officer Collins, when you are done tormenting me, would you please find Lieutenant Berger and ask him if he could swing back here? I would normally track him down myself, but I think it best if I don't put too much pressure on this for the moment," she motioned at the now mostly wrapped leg, "wouldn't you agree?"

Collins finished pinning the bandage in place and looked up at the pallid Chief. "Yes, ma'am, I would." She closed her bag and stood. "I'll send him back this way," she said, and headed up the street. The three, armed squad members forming a perimeter around the approach to the entrance ignored her as she passed, keeping their attention on the mine itself.

Fran turned back to her.

"It's going to get ugly, Holly."

She surprised herself with a full-throated laugh.

"As opposed to the picnic so far?" She stepped up to Fran and slid her arm around her. They had to get away from the mine entrance in case the Tierney-Hotchkins creature decided it was time to leave its nest.

She led Hopper around the hill outside, a few yards from the opening. When she released her arm from Fran's waist, Hopper gave Holly's hand a brief squeeze, surprising and warming the deputy.

The Chief propped herself against the outer embankment.

Before they could continue the conversation, Berger appeared from around the corner of Main Street and made his way to them.

He acknowledged her and spoke to Hopper. "My folks have positions at key spots to prevent anyone from leaving town, even if they break through and leave the mine. I also took the liberty of contacting your dispatcher and, under your authority, asked the remaining members of your force to meet and coordinate with the two officers I have stationed back at the main road turn-in."

Some might have viewed it as a power move, undercutting Hopper's authority over her own people, but she knew it wasn't. Berger was verifying with the Chief that she was good with his action, and she was sure he would rescind it immediately if Hopper gave any sign that she wasn't. He might officially outrank her, but this was a sergeant checking with his lieutenant to ensure his actions had been in accordance with her wishes, not a trooper informing a local cop of what the Staties had decided.

"Thanks, Jim," Hopper said. "What's the armament situation?"

"Aside from standard sidearms, officially we've got Colt long-barrels, flashbangs, scatter guns, and two MP5s."

The latter, she knew, were fully automatic submachine guns. Much more substantial an arsenal than the Prescott force would normally have available, but she privately questioned if even it would be sufficient under the circumstances.

Apparently, Hopper agreed with her. The wounded woman frowned and said, "Ok, it will have to do. You have how many?"

"Nine plus me."

"Check." The Chief seemed to be running through an inventory list in her head, comparing it against whatever it was she had in mind. "There should be at least half a dozen of my folks on their way to meet yours at the road. Once they are there, have the group split into two squads, staggered. One stays with the cruisers, the other sets up a hundred yards or so in by the road, clear sightlines toward Warner."

"Roger that," Berger responded. "And the rest of us?"

"Augment the three on the close perimeter with the three you have around on Main. Those flashbangs...wait. You said *officially*." She peered at Berger and the man somehow conveyed a look both of innocence and amusement.

He chuckled, "Thought you were slipping for a minute, Fran. We might have a few extra pieces with us. You know how things collect over time and you forget about them."

Holly had missed the *official* in his earlier statement and part of her was aghast that Berger was admitting to having unauthorized weapons in his possession.

Mostly, though, she was relieved that they weren't quite as limited as she had feared. Whatever the hell was in the mine, she thought the submachine gun, which used similar ammo to their Glock sidearms, wouldn't do much other than piss the thing off.

"Uh huh," Hopper said. "What exactly has been collecting dust in your bag of tricks?"

"A few frags that somehow got mixed in with the flashbangs plus a couple of small launchers with a dozen, maybe a dozen and a half rounds."

Holy shit.

The fragmentation grenades were capable of tearing a target apart, although Holly knew that with this creature, nothing was guaranteed.

"Some things never change." Hopper shook her head, but Holly saw a pleased look that belied any criticism Berger might have inferred from the motion. "Thankfully. Ok, we'll want those with the mine perimeter folks."

"You are slipping, Fran. You're still one short."

"The medic, you mean? I assumed you would keep her back and at the ready."

"Collins is our medic," he agreed. "But that's just 'other duties as assigned'. She's fully qualified and is going to be mightily pissed if she is left out of things. Major pain in my ass, which I've told her, but she qualifies every way to Sunday."

This garnered a sideways look at her from Hopper as the Chief said, "Yeah, I'm familiar. Fine, put her with the perimeter team. And give a launcher to whoever has the highest marksmanship.

"That would be Collins. And the three of us?"

She held her breath, waiting for what she was afraid would be the reply.

"We're going back in."

Corporeal!

It relished the feel of the bodies as its claws tore through carcasses of the former vessels, the cooling blood and flesh barely taking the edge off its immense hunger. But there would be warm meat soon enough.

Finishing what had once been an insurance agent, it stretched to its full height, towering over the now empty frame. Chitinous talons clicked together as it sucked in the flat air of the cavern.

The water behind it no longer shone. All the energy gained through its proxy feeding and ceremony had been spent when it burst through the vellum, piercing the veil back into this world.

And without the essence of the black woman, there was nothing left to energize its former prison to feed into Prescott's water supply.

No matter. It had no doubt there would be another attempt to stop it shortly. There would be sufficient blood to slake not only its current thirst but to ensure the entire town stood ready to serve and act as the vanguard for its spread across the land.

A scaly, bow-legged step and it stood over the former waitress from the Twisted Kitty. With a quick 'snap' the marrow in the creature's leg bone was exposed, and it sucked at the morsel, savoring the thought of what was to come.

Yes, now was its time. With its foe having no knowledge of the ancient ways that could have been used to stall or keep it from its course, there was nothing to prevent it from turning the entire world into its personal feeding ground. Then, it would select a new nesting place and bring forth additional Fomórach, all subservient to itself. Yes, there were still some of the cattle with an ability to ignore or fight off its influence but, again, no matter. Without the primordial words of power, it could not be defeated.

It ripped an arm free from the carcass at its horned feet and used the jagged bone end to pick at a string of meat between two of its primary teeth.

It sat back on its haunches and waited.

"An invisible demon used magic and human skin to somehow merge two people, including the guy suspected of the murders at the Twisted Kitty, your officer, and the coroner, then to create a giant lizard body out of thin air. Oh, and it has an extra mouth. I have that right?"

They were just outside the opening to shaft three, doing a final run-through of the plan before re-entering the mine.

"Yeah, that about sums it up, Jim," Hopper replied. "Any other questions?"

"No, I think that about covers it." Berger checked the action on the grenade launcher in his hands, patted his vest where three additional grenade rounds were hanging. "I should have known it would be extra interesting when I got word it was you, Fran." He peered at her. "I'm assuming, of course, that you haven't finally gone bat-shit crazy?" The question sounded half hopeful.

"Nope, but if it makes you feel better, just pretend it's a heavily armed and fortified serial killer in there." She pointed to the launcher. "And I think you had an inkling," she said, referring to his comment about an interesting time. "You brought party favors, after all."

"Even I can learn a few lessons, if I'm hit in the head enough times," he said. He gave a little nod for Hopper to take the lead.

Hopper said, "Good to know," and limped forward, a crutch under one arm to keep weight off her damaged leg and knee.

Holly had initially felt a bit of a third wheel at the easy banter between Fran and Berger but realized she was being silly and clamped down on it. They had been through a different kind of hell together and the man obviously respected Hopper as much as she did. When he turned to make sure she was all set as the rearguard, Holly managed a small smile toward him and got one in return. She adjusted the automatic M4 supplied by Berger and followed the trooper through the entrance, a launcher riding easily on his shoulder. He had gotten word from his people out at the road that half a dozen Prescott officers were now present, and the combined group had taken position per Hopper's request. The remaining troopers had spread out in a semi-circle twenty yards back on the street outside the mine, long rifles aimed at the entrance. Holly had seen Collins laying prone, attaching the other launcher to the top of a small tripod when they passed on the way to the mine entrance.

A few feet inside the entrance, Hopper paused.

"Jim? I assume you didn't share my version of things with your people. What are they expecting?"

There was a derisive sound from the trooper. "Not a chance. I told them there is a group of heavily armed and desperate confirmed killers in the mine that are hell-bent on taking as many as they can with them if it comes down to it."

"And?" The Chief pressed him.

He blew out his breath. "And, as you requested, I told them that if anyone except us pokes their heads into view from the mine, they are to lay down suppressing fire while Collins brings the shaft down around their ears. Regardless if we're out or not."

Hopper said quietly, nodding, "I'm sure they were not particularly pleased with that."

The tone of the response was explosive, albeit in a matching quiet voice. "For fuck's sake, of course not. It took a few minutes to drill it into them that it wasn't negotiable and that if they didn't follow orders and I did make it out, I would make sure they spent the next ten years writing tickets to moose in northern Alaska. In Collins's case, I thought I was going to have to club her but, in the end, even she agreed."

Berger seemed ready to move on, but Hopper continued. "What about you, Jim?"

He faced the Chief. "What about me, Fran? Do you mean, 'do I like it?' Of course not. But from what you've told me, it's the only play. It's just... this isn't the type of thing any of my people have ever dealt with." There was no sense of doubt or even resentment over the possible outcome for him personally. His anger was centered on the impact on his people.

I can see why they get along so well.

"I understand," the Chief said, and brushed his sleeve with her hand.

Berger gave a slight grunt but said nothing more.

They turned into the darkness.

It knew much that the humans had either forgotten or had never known. How its kind had stumbled across this world, having depleted all other realms they had traveled through, finding sustenance beyond anything previously encountered. The flesh of the bipeds that inhabited a small portion of the planet was, unto itself, well enough, but the depth of emotions, of pain, went beyond anything they had yet encountered. It was decided that this sphere would be their permanent home, and each Fomórach had laid claim to a populated zone of the verdant world.

And all was well for many eons.

Then, as the natives developed and spread from their savannah homeland, the internecine battles began between the Fomórach, each fighting for a greater share of the unparalleled bounty.

Until only it remained.

Crossing mountains and oceans and sampling the delicacy offered by the now planet-wide creatures, it finally settled on a northern peninsula that became an island shortly after its arrival. While not an immediate need, it knew it would have to create its own progeny and therefore performed the anchoring ceremony to the island, preparatory to its future nesting.

And, again, all was well.

But over time, the primitive creatures continued to change. They learned to harness some of the same power that had allowed the Fomórach to travel between spheres. Then the painted invaders arrived on its island, and it found itself dispersed, almost powerless, far from its chosen nesting place.

But since the time of its banishment, they had forgotten. What they called 'science' had opened small understandings into some of the most obvious aspects of the world around them, but in the process of gaining these understandings, they had lost the knowledge of the connections between all things, seen and unseen.

Thus, their loss would lead to their resubmission to it, as its herd. And with their numbers now so large, it would be able to indulge its deepest hungers without fear of over-culling.

It raised its head and sniffed.

They approached. And limited as its physical senses were, a minor drawback to having returned fully to this realm, it tasted a whiff of the dark woman that had escaped.

Good. Her blood would soon course across the stones and bring its essence to the others in the town.

Chapter 17

On the surface, the plan sounded similar to the one she had laid out earlier before the Meredith Baxter rescue attempt. And Hopper was more than aware of how that had ended.

This time, however, she and her two companions knew up front that anything they ran into was a hostile, to be taken out on sight.

She wished she had time to talk to Holly. She wouldn't apologize for dragging her into the situation. The younger woman was well aware of what they were facing, and an apology would come across as a diminishment of the newly deputized woman's bravery, regardless of how she meant it.

But she would tell Holly she was honored to have her at her side during what was to come. Under other circumstances...

Enough of that, she scolded herself.

The cubby where Baxter had lain in wait with her false pleas, and Miller's shallow dugout, was just ahead.

As was Larry's body, his face almost unrecognizable with the metal spike protruding through its center.

She offered a silent prayer to whatever positive forces might be listening as she swung her crutch around him and stepped past his corpse. As she did, she gestured with her sidearm toward the fallen cop's holster. Berger paused long enough to pull out the Glock and shove it into his waistband.

The earlier glow from the cavern was gone, and the muted pre-sunrise light from outside faded. She paused and pulled down her night vision goggles, and the trooper and Holly followed suit.

The cavern opening was just ahead.

Once again, Holly was not pleased with the Chief's plan, although she couldn't disagree with the general concept. They were flying blind, and she was certain that Fran's training and experience, as deep as it was, didn't include how to deal with a multi-mouthed hell-demon any more than her own did.

What about Karz?

She pushed the thought aside for later consideration.

Fran had a hunch that whatever the creature was, it now had a hard-on for her, based on the rather violent bow-out she had done from its earlier plans.

Holly didn't doubt that. What she did doubt was the wisdom of letting the Chief, particularly in her severely wounded state, act as bait.

Again.

Hopper planned on drawing the demon out into a position that would give Berger a chance to put a grenade or two down its dual mouths.

Her own role was, if possible, to keep Fran out of its claws and distract it as necessary until the state trooper could line up a reasonable shot.

The fallback plan was to use the launcher to bring the cavern ceiling down on top of it. And them.

She strongly suspected the fallback would be necessary but took some solace in that between collapsing the cavern itself and the troopers stationed outside being ready to seal the main entrance if the three of them didn't make it out, the creature would hopefully be killed, or at least permanently trapped.

Although there wasn't much about any of the current circumstances that lent itself to hope, she was optimistic by nature. At the moment, though, she had to force herself to locate a bright spot.

I made deputy. There is that. Although outside of Berger, who will also probably die a horrible and painful death, no one else knows. Besides, aside from Mom and Dad, who else would I brag to? Lauren? That was over, even if her former girlfriend ever bothered to call.

She had an image of sitting in front of a roaring fire, sharing a drink with Fran Hopper, talking about the day's happenings at the station.

Stop. That isn't going to happen, even if you do get out of this intact. She's the Chief, and besides, she's never given any indication of interest.

Damn it.

The loose stone ramp was just ahead of Hopper and the three of them halted at the same time.

The throbbing hum in her head was back, threatening to block out other thoughts and sounds. She shook her head and saw Berger doing the same thing just ahead of her. Hopper seemed to not notice it. The Chief turned to them and motioned toward the sides of the tunnel.

She took a position across from the trooper. The Chief remained in the middle of the shaft.

No speaking now. They didn't need signals since the plan itself was essentially Fran acting as chum in the water for the hell-beast, while Holly played wing-woman.

With the crutch for balance, Hopper made her way up the ramp, her somewhat clumsy movement at odds with the smooth, gracefulness Holly was used to seeing. She watched the Chief duck slightly as she passed through the opening and descended the other side. She and Berger followed.

It took a moment for Hopper to get her footing at the bottom of the ramp, then Holly moved a dozen paces to the side, taking up a position against the cavern wall. Berger hung back.

The plastic framework was still in place, its center now empty. On either side of it were the remains of what had once been walking, talking humans, and she swallowed heavily. Signs of their existence were now limited to torn fragments of flesh and broken pieces of bone sitting in thickening pools of blood.

In the midst of the remains sat the creature, reclining on heavily muscled and scaled hind legs, as though waiting for a netherworld bus. It had raised its head at their entrance, second mouth protruding, fangs opening and dripping as the Chief and she took their positions, but otherwise it hadn't moved.

"Hey? Shit-mouth! I'm back!"

The call from Fran was expected. What wasn't was the Chief tossing her crutch to the side and taking a slow limping step forward, toward the beast.

As much as she wanted to, she didn't call out. Her trust in Fran was complete. Besides, the Chief was going to do what she was going to do, period.

She reached down and made sure the snap on her sidearm holster was open before returning her hand to the rifle. She pulled the Colt up into firing position and waited.

There was no visible reaction from the beast, but the pounding in her head increased. Even Hopper seemed to be affected this time, cocking her head to the side, but then continued her taunts.

"Pretty weak, if you ask me. You a hell-beast or some kind of snaggle-toothed possum-weasel?"

Watching both her Chief and the beast, she took a lurching step forward.

The pressure in Holly's head increased and if she had been able to, she would have yelled, but she couldn't spare the energy. There was an attractive whisper underlying the pressure, and she felt an urge to drop the rifle.

Or turn its aim on Hopper.

Not happening.

She *pushed* as hard as she could inside her head, and the whisper dissipated. She caught a hint of frustration, *or possibly surprise?* as it did.

Fuck you.

There was no doubt that the thing in front of them was trying to infiltrate her mind. Her being. And she also had no doubt what would happen if she allowed it to.

She kept her aim on the beast as Hopper hobbled slightly closer to it.

"Yo, you even listening? Warner is in my jurisdiction. And last I checked, ugly otherworldly critters are against the law hereabouts. You want to leave peacefully, or do I have to take you in?"

She doubted it was the words themselves that set the beast off, if the creature even understood them. But the taunting, belittling tone transcended language and perhaps dimensions.

The head rose toward the cavern roof, propelled by plated legs. The mouths opened and a piercing sound reverberated around the chamber.

She felt wetness seep from her ears and saw blood trickling from Hopper's. She took a step back.

"Christ on a stick, you're one tricky lizard, aren't you? Tell you what, instead of the usual 'three hundred or thirty days' I'll let you off with a warning to stay the fuck out of my dimension if you toddle off to whatever hell-world you came from right now. Deal?"

She watched Hopper slide her Glock from her holster, and braced the rifle against her shoulder, hoping Berger was ready.

The invisible stabbing in her ears and head stopped, but she was wary of any change in the environment. Her suspicion was proven right when the massive creature turned toward Hopper and began moving.

It took only a single step, though, then stopped.

She caught something in her periphery vision and assumed Berger was moving into position.

Thweet!

She whirled to see Berger with his sidearm out, aimed not at the creature, but at Hopper.

The rifle dropped from her hands, and she sprinted toward him. Hopper twisted as a bullet passed through her upper arm. Before he could squeeze off another round, she was on him, one arm slamming down on his gun, the other extended palm forward, coming in hard against the side of his head.

Both the gun and the trooper dropped, and her leg, tucked under her when she had launched herself, unbent just enough to allow the knee to slam into his chest, adding momentum to his trip to the ground.

His eyes looked blindly and cloudily up when she pinned him. She brought her right hand across to a backhand and brought it down in a wicked slap across his face. When there was no change in his expression, she reversed the blow, leaving a bright red mark on the other cheek.

Still no reaction. She used two fingers and jabbed him just above the collarbone. His eyes flashed with pain, then cleared a bit before hazing over once more. She used her fingers again, this time applying pressure to the side of his neck just under the jawline, and he yelled, trying to shake her off. She held on, yelling his name. He shook for a few more seconds, then stopped, looking up at her in confusion.

"Willingham?"

"Berger! It's fucking with your head." When he shook his head again uncertainly, she added, "Hopper needs us!"

He blinked heavily. She was afraid she had lost him again when he opened his eyes and dipped his head.

The creature screamed.

She glanced behind her to see the Chief hopping, trying to put more distance between herself and the pissed off, howling demon.

"Got it. I'm...I'm all right. Jesus, what is that thing?"

She gave him a hard look before swinging her leg over him.

"No idea. But if we do our jobs, it will be dead shortly. Where's the launcher?"

He was on his feet. "Back by the entrance. I dropped it when...when it told me to—"

"All right." She wasn't going to push him on what had happened. It could have just as easily been her. It *had* been her earlier, in fact.

"Grab it," she said, then ignored him. The thing was moving again, heading toward Hopper, who was now backed against the cavern wall.

Shit.

She shouted, "Hey! Fuck-face! Over here!"

She continued screaming and waving her arms as she danced sideways toward the rifle, trying to keep the demon's attention.

It pivoted its craggy maw in her direction and let out another shriek as she scooped the rifle up.

The M4 was comforting in her grasp, illusionary as she knew that feeling was. Her father had always told her she had an innate sense of aim and direction, and she hoped that held true even in this, the worst of circumstances.

She opened fire in three second bursts, the staccato sound of the bullets dampening the continued hum in her head. She started at the beast's double-knees and slowly moved her aim up to the extended second mouth that seemed to strain against the tendons tethering it to the demon's body.

Teeth shattered, fragments hitting the floor stones. Ripples appeared in the water behind it as shards flew into the lake.

The shriek was now a roar and the air once again seemed to shimmer, power vibrating the ether into and around her, shoving her slightly backwards. It took another shambling step toward her, then another.

She caught movement out of the corner of her eye. It was Berger, the launcher hanging down his back. She thought Hopper would have been familiar with the look in his eyes as he fired the Glock handgun in a steady, repetitive motion, targeting whatever weak spots he saw in their adversary.

She was glad he was back to himself and on their team.

Her finger continued squeezing the trigger. On. Off. On. Off. Over and over until the magazine was empty.

Then, without looking away from her target, she jettisoned the empty, slid her hand into her pocket, pulled out the spare clip, and slammed it into position.

She recommenced firing; it had taken her no more than three seconds to reload.

Black liquid, pooling like a thick syrup, appeared in the pock-marked holes scattered across the creature's body.

Another roar told her she had pissed it off even more than it already had been.

Works for me.

It was now ignoring Hopper, who was still up against the cave wall and seemed to be fumbling in her pocket for something.

She needed to make sure it was fully engaged and enraged, so Berger would have a clear shot at its mouth.

One of them, at least.

None of them knew for sure what it would take to kill it. The working premise was a shot into its head, assuming its brain was stored there. If it wasn't...well, they would cross that particular nightmare if they came to it.

Admit it. If it isn't, we're fucked. Big time.

But that was the reason for the backup plan. And the backup to the backup plan, the troopers outside on the ready to bring down the whole dig around their ears.

She leaped to her right as the creature made its way toward her.

Berger, now holding the launcher, was still behind both her and Hopper but had moved over to her other side, closer to the Chief. He moved again, adjusting his position, trying to get and keep a clear line to the beast.

"Come on, you scaly fuckety-fuck!" She waved her rifle over her head as it wavered between continuing its pursuit of her and going after the Chief.

She let off another burst, aware that she would shortly be out of ammo.

"Holly! Live round!"

Her head swung toward Hopper, who threw something her way.

A grenade. She stepped toward the Chief, grabbed the small globe in flight and underhanded it at the feet of the creature that was getting a bit too close to her for comfort.

There was a *whoomph* as she ducked and covered her head to shield it from flying stones.

When she looked up again, she saw the demon leaning back, disoriented from the blast but apparently uninjured. It opened its mouths and let out the loudest shriek yet, and she felt more wetness trickling from her ears.

We are so fucked.

Just then, Berger ran ahead of her, raised the launcher, sighted through the small metal rectangle on top, and sent a rocket grenade directly toward the open second mouth.

Yes!

Sparks followed the hissing round as it cleared the parted, broken teeth and exploded, rocking the beast back on its haunches where it hung for a moment before falling to the stones.

Holly ran forward, squeezing off rounds at its head as she did.

Another rocket grenade whooshed by her and tore off part of the side of its face. Berger joined her as she approached the fallen hell-creature and waved her back. Keeping back a dozen yards himself, he then launched another rocket into the creature's head, followed by the final two in his vest. These opened more of the hell-beast's head and skull. He then dropped the launcher and began firing with his sidearm. She stepped up and joined him, changing her previous intermittent bursts to a continuous stream of bullets, all aimed up through the damaged open mouth and face, where she hoped they would ricochet through the skull and do mortal damage.

Berger screamed.

"Die, you cock-sucking monster!"

Her rifle clicked dry a few seconds before his Glock did and they both reached into pockets to bring out their last remaining ammunition.

"It's dead."

The statement wasn't shouted but the voice, and tone, cut through both of their battle fog.

Their heads turned toward the pallid Prescott Chief of Police, who was limping heavily toward them.

"It's dead," Hopper repeated.

Eyes back to the supine beast laying before them. More of its head lay in pieces around it than were attached to its body.

"Dead?" She felt foolish as she spoke, but the adrenaline had yet to taper off.

Fran, standing next to the thing's head, leaned over and poked it with a finger.

"Yep. You did it."

It still hadn't sunk in, but she tried to digest the words.

"Dead." It was a statement this time, and she stepped up to the monstrosity, staring down at it. Steam started to seep from between its scales and out of the decimated skull.

She kicked it.

Still nothing. She also realized that there was no humming, no *pushing* feeling in her head.

She turned toward Hopper.

"It's dead."

"That would be an accurate description, deputy." Hopper said with extreme seriousness.

"Fran…"

It was Berger.

"Fran, I'm sorry."

The former Army Lieutenant shrugged and smiled. "No problem, Jim. Shit happens. And–"

"Usually, it happens to us," he finished, apparently picking up on an old joke.

Returning to the topic, he went on doggedly. "Really. I don't know what happened. It was like something was hitting my brain with electric shocks, turning me into a trained monkey."

Hopper shook her head, still not accepting there was anything to apologize for.

"Trust me, you have never been particularly well trained. And for once, I'm thankful for that." She gave him a full-blown smile, and he returned it.

"Now if one of you wouldn't mind, I surely could use a hand getting out of this God forsaken cave. I'm about done in."

Before Berger could move, she jumped forward and slid her arm around her Chief.

"I've got you, Fran."

"Thank you, Holly," Hopper said gently, looking at her. She slid her own arm around the deputy's waist.

Holly felt the blood rushing to her cheeks and didn't care.

The troopers manning the shaft perimeter shouted a warning, which Berger responded to immediately.

Holly thought it would really suck if they were taken out by friendly fire after all that had happened.

Outside the mine entrance, the sky above the surrounding forest was dark pink, bordering on blue.

When Holly half-carried Fran Hopper out into the open, Officer Collins immediately ran forward with a med kit in hand.

"Stretcher, now!" Collins shouted without turning around. She popped open the bag and pulled out a loaded hypo.

Before the Chief could argue, the diminutive trooper said, "Shut it, Chief Hopper. This is going into you one way or another." Excess liquid spouted from the needle's tip as the medic verified the dose.

Hopper simply said, "Yes, ma'am," and held out her good arm.

Collins jabbed the needle into the proffered appendage, giving a dirty look as she noticed the blood seeping through the sleeve of the other arm.

"Sorry about that, Officer Collins. I tried to avoid making any extra work for you, but sometimes…"

Collins, apparently having studied under Berger for an extended period, replied in a resigned mutter, "shit happens and usually, it happens to you." Shaking her head, she pulled out a pair of surgical scissors, and cut away the shirt around Hopper's newest wound.

Berger was standing next to Holly and Hopper. The three looked at each other and smiled.

CHAPTER 18

"I really should be back at my place."

It was a comment Fran Hopper had made, at a minimum, once a day for the last two weeks. The Prescott Chief of Police, currently on sick leave, sat perched up in the queen bed, a down comforter laying lightly across her lap. A tray with sliced fruits and vegetables in small pseudo-oriental decorated bowls was on her lap.

The town's newest deputy ignored the comment and took the empty tissue box into the kitchen for disposal.

Holly had been slightly hurt when she first heard Fran say it, but had gotten past it. That had been the day before Hopper was discharged from the county hospital, following three surgeries and five weeks of recuperation in a private room. Technically, she should have been in a shared room, but Berger, with the backing of the entire Prescott police force, had emphatically informed the hospital administrator *'fuck the insurance'* and then pointed out that patrols into the administrator's high-end housing development could easily be eliminated. This quickly resulted in Hopper being moved into what amounted to a suite consisting of two connecting rooms; Berger and Holly alternated sleeping in the empty one during Hopper's lengthy stay.

She had been sitting in the chair next to Hopper's bed, Berger on the other side, as her friend mentioned hiring a temporary aide to help her around her apartment.

Holly, somewhat tentatively and feeling her cheeks flush, suggested completing the convalescence at Holly's apartment, where Holly would be more than happy to help take care of her. Berger immediately heartily seconded the idea. Fran's response, preceded by '*That is very kind of you, Deputy, but...*' was so polite and formal sounding that after Holly had nodded understandingly, she excused herself, said she needed a drink, and quickly headed down the hall to the family waiting room, just getting inside before the tears started to fall.

She had mentally kicked herself for making the offer. Granted, the doctor had said it would be at least a few weeks before the Chief should put any pressure on her leg and replacement knee, but Holly's apartment was a second-story walk up while Fran's was ground level. Logistically and logically, it didn't make sense.

Jim Berger appeared in the waiting room doorway. She was going to brush him off, but he didn't give her a chance.

"Willingham, you need to understand something. I won't say I know everything about her, but I know *her*, you know?" He waited until she nodded in acknowledgement. "I think you know her pretty much too, at this point. What you have to understand is she's a centurion."

"What?" Whatever she might have expected him to come out with, that wasn't even on the list.

He gave a self-deprecating laugh. "Sorry, I pulled a B.A. in ancient history before I did my hitch. It's–"

"I know what a centurion is," she said, miffed and still confused. "But I don't understand what you mean about Fran."

He took a deep breath before continuing. "If the barbarians are at the gate, you wouldn't want anyone else at your side. She would lock arms with you and face whatever the horde threw at you. Hell, she would be out in front, you know that. And if she was taken down by a spear, she would accept, expect, you to drag her out of harm's way, same as she would do for you. If you needed someone to lead a platoon over the hill through no-man's-land to take out a gunner's nest, she would be right in front, doing her damnedest to get everyone through."

She had snuffed and said, "I *know* that. Christ, of course I do."

"Yeah, but that's not this," he said. "This isn't dragging a ruined leg through a cavern, teasing a demon's attention to give us a one in a thousand chance to kill it before it took out Prescott and however many others it planned."

His voice dropped.

"This is peace. And I'm not sure she has ever had that, at least since Afghanistan."

She looked at him.

"Look, I'm not saying she's a cyborg. She feels, too much I think sometimes. That's part of it. Normally, she can't allow herself to, so she stuffs the emotions down into a box. Otherwise, it would keep her from doing what she has to do."

She was quiet for a moment, then asked. "Jim, what happened on that run to Karz?"

He gave her a considering look. Then, "That's something you'll have to get Fran to tell you. And if you can, you'll know you've gotten through."

"The good news," he gave her a half-smile, "is that you'll have plenty of time to work on her when she's recuperating at your place."

"But she said no."

He smiled. "Sure, she did. But if you ignore it, and simply go ahead with the plan, I guarantee she won't squawk. Much."

He left the waiting room and headed back to say goodbye to the patient.

So she knew the latest utterance by her roommate was simply a reflex and didn't let it faze her.

She returned to the bedroom and stood in the doorway, looking at Fran. The police chief looked back guiltily.

"Holly, really. I'm sorry to be such a bother. There's no reason–"

"Can it, Fran."

The thought of speaking to her Chief a month ago in that manner would not have even crossed her mind. If someone had even suggested it, she would have reamed them a new one.

But that was then.

She smiled at Fran and checked the tray on the bed next to her, doing a quick mental comparison between the lunch she had delivered an hour before and what was on the tray now.

Not a lot, but enough. I'll save a scolding for another time.

She moved the tray to the nightstand and walked around to the vacant side of the bed.

She pulled the covers back, kicked off her slippers and climbed into the bed. One arm slid around the other woman who sighed and leaned against her shoulder.

"No, I mean it. I–"

She kissed the top of Fran's head, still slightly surprised at the softness of the cropped curls. "I said don't start. Another ten days and, assuming Doctor Jenkins gives you a clean bill of health, you don't ever have to see me again." A wry smile. "Unless you work late, of course."

"Damn you." Hopper snuggled her head harder against her. "I still don't know how to handle this. In the service–"

"We're not in the service," she reminded her yet again. "And yes, there are some department regs we - note I said *we* - need to figure out how to handle, but we will. If I need to transfer, or get a different job, so be it."

Perspective was a funny thing. At this point, even with the field promotion to deputy, being a cop wasn't as important as it had been a short time before.

Another sigh from her lover, who snuggled back against her. "Yes, ma'am."

She couldn't help but smile. "I sort of like the sound of that."

There was a rumbling grumble in her armpit. "Don't get used to it, deputy."

She laughed outright, now. "Oh, I won't. Yet."

Her hand stroked Fran's head, and she leaned her own against it, thinking how odd the world was.

Warner was cordoned off, with enough warnings posted at the county road turnoff, around the town itself, and at the sealed shaft three, the latter courtesy of Collins after she once again traded her med kit for the grenade launcher, to keep even the most intrepid teenager at bay. Fred and Larry and the remains of the other victims, along with those from the Twisted Kitty, had been sent to the Morgantown Medical

Examiner Office and were awaiting final disposition. There had been questions, of course, both from Prescott's town leaders and from Jim Berger's superiors, but with the cavern and outer mine entrance sealed, the collective story by Hopper, Berger, and herself regarding a group of deranged addicts with explosives committing the murders, kidnapping the Chamber President along with a well-regarded retired insurance broker before they inadvertently blew themselves up was sufficient to, if not totally satisfy everyone, at least settle things down. She believed, or at least hoped, it would fade into Prescott lore over time, perhaps claiming a spot next to the mostly unspoken legends of Warner itself.

Poor Carl, she thought again. *And Meredith. Even Bird and Tierney. They didn't ask for any of it. Of course, neither did we.*

She looked down at Fran's braced leg and stroked the other's cheek.

And talk about odd. Here she was nuzzling with a woman that, until a short time ago, had intimidated her so much that she had a hard time responding to her in a straight sentence.

I'll take it.

A quiet period passed in contented silence, then she grunted.

"Whoof!"

A large ball of fur sat purring on her stomach.

"Bad, Mr. Whiskers! You know better!"

Fran chuckled and reached out a hand to scratch the cat's ear as she addressed the interloper.

"Don't mind her, Whiskers. We both know how much a softy she is."

She stuck her tongue out at the comment but joined Fran in petting the cat. For his part, Mr. Whiskers deigned to allow the ministrations, and arched his back in a sign of pleasure.

After a few minutes of this, the feline put his face up against hers, nudging at her.

"Apparently, his highness has decided it's time for dinner. Will you be ok for a bit?"

Fran smiled. "Yeah. I need to do some leg lifts, so I don't get grief from Jenkins at my next appointment. Go take care of the furry dictator."

They kissed, and she got out of bed, sliding back into the slippers Hopper had declared were 'improbably cute', bunny faces adorning each.

She paused at the bedroom doorway.

"Fran? What happened in Karz?"

The huge smile she had on her face when she left the room caused Fran to give her a strange look, but she didn't care.

Without hesitation, Fran Hopper had replied, "I'll tell you tonight after dinner."

Hopper did ten repetitions with her healing leg, keeping it straight as the physical therapist had instructed, then did ten with her undamaged one, for good measure. She repeated the sequence three more times and laid her head back on the pillow, slightly out of breath.

Damn it, this is ridiculous.

Actually, the entire situation was a bit absurd. She was, essentially, shacked up with a white girl who, while not young enough to be her daughter, had at least a passing shot at being mistaken for a niece, assuming her family was easy going and integrated. The department issues she wasn't as concerned about as Holly thought. Explaining to her father, a man who had taken several years to come to grips with her being gay, that was a different matter.

Christ on a stick.

But one thing at a time. The fact was, she was very fond of Holly. Perhaps too fond for her own good. She hadn't been in a real relationship since before her first deployment, and how that one had ended still stung if she allowed herself to think about it.

She and the deputy had started sleeping together a few nights after Holly had carried her up the stairs to her apartment. It had reminded her of some old movie where the groom lifted his new bride over the threshold of their house. Apparently, the same thought had crossed Holly's mind. They entered the apartment, and the younger woman sat her gently down on the living room sofa, declaring with a grin, "Honey, we're home."

It could be handy having skin the color of ebony at times like those; she doubted the deputy had detected her blush.

But she had felt it, damn it. She knew she shouldn't be here. It wasn't proper.

Really, Fran? You're going with proper? You can do better than that at rationalizing.

The voice in her head sounded suspiciously like Jim Berger's, who had checked in a couple of times a week since their demon-spelunking adventure. She had never quite caught him smirking during those visits, when Holly solicitously straightened her pillows, brought her a snack, or kissed the top of her head. But she was sure he was enjoying her discomfort.

She sighed. It was obvious he was glad that she had someone taking care of her who so obviously cared about her as much as he did.

Friends. What a pain in the ass.

Exercises done, she closed her eyes and dozed off. When she woke, her hand reached to the empty pillow beside her. She wasn't sure how long she had napped, but it certainly had been longer than it took to dump a can of tuna into Mr. Whiskers' bowl or even empty his litter box.

She wondered if Holly had gone shopping and hoped she would return soon, wanting the warmth of the other woman, and not just of her body next to hers, to keep her company.

Jesus, you're getting soft. Give her a break. She's been going to work and spending the rest of her time taking care of your sorry ass.

Regardless, she lifted her splinted leg and swung it outward. She shuffled her butt over and set her legs on the floor. The ever-present crutch was next to the nightstand, and she used it to pull herself up.

"Holly? Mr. Whiskers giving you grief? I was thinking we might watch that last Die-Hard movie you said you haven't seen, if you're up for it. Then later I can tell you a bedtime story involving me, a pain in the ass sergeant, and a small Afghan town called Karz." She made her way to the doorway and stepped out into the hall.

No answer.

She continued down the hallway, past the bathroom. As she did, she thought she heard rustling in the kitchen and wondered if the cat had gotten into his bag of food.

"Holly?"

She cursed the crutch she had to continue using for the next two weeks and thought back to a few days before, when she had informed her caretaker that she was certain the crutch must have formed a callous by now. The other, with mock seriousness, had insisted on performing an examination which resulted in additional laughter along with other unrelated activities. Later, sated and drowsy, Holly had told her that her skin was as soft and smooth as ever.

Yeah, a bit more than fond of her.

She repeated her call as she stepped into the kitchen.

No....

The table that served as the dining room in the oversized kitchen was covered in a sheen of red, thick strings of it hanging over the edges with an occasional blurping drip to the floor. Tufts of fur dotted the dinosaur-shaped salt and pepper shakers, and there was a large knife standing upright in the tabletop. Its tip was hidden from view through the carcass pinned to the wood.

The woman that had been her lover and nurse and perhaps, in a future that would now never come to be, something more, looked up from the half-eaten skull in her hands and smiled.

One of the first things Fran Hopper had noticed about the young woman applying for the overnight dispatcher job had been her white, even teeth. These were gone now, in their place small, edged, and pointed ones poked out from mottled red and black gums.

The woman pulled the knife free from the table and stood.

"Hi Fran. No worries, it's all good."

About the Author

Born on a sweltering August morning in the grittiest city in the U.S., Neil T. Jacobs began life as he has continued to live it, more than a little annoyed and wondering what all the bother is about.

His significant life experiences include... well, the statute of limitations hasn't expired in at least a few cases, so let's just leave it at 'He's been around'.

www.neiltjacobs.com

SEE ME

• •

A NOVEL

RHODA BERLIN

What's Next
Washington

Publisher's Note: This is a work of fiction. Names, characters, places, businesses, and incidents are products of the author's imagination or are used fictitiously. Locales and public names are sometimes used for atmospheric purposes. Any resemblance to actual people, living or dead, or to events, institutions, or places is completely coincidental.

Author's Note: I delighted in fully personalizing *See Me*. If you're curious as to the form this took, a hint's on my website: https://rhodaberlin.com/fun-stuff

Book Layout ©2024 BookDesignTemplates.com
Cover Design and Author Photograph by Cybil Flores

See Me / Rhoda Berlin.
ISBN 979-8-9898938-0-5 (pbk.)
ISBN 979-8-9898938-1-2 (ebook)